DANNY ORLIS
AND THE
ICE FISHING ESCAPADE

DANNY ORLIS

AND THE

ICE FISHING ESCAPADE

BERNARD PALMER

Danny Orlis and the Ice Fishing Escapade
© 2024 by Bernard Palmer
All rights reserved. First edition 1964.
Second edition 2024.

Scripture quotations from The Authorized (King James) Version. Rights in the Authorized Version in the United Kingdom are vested in the Crown. Reproduced by permission of the Crown's patentee, Cambridge University Press.

Cover image: Adobe Firefly
Character illustrations: John Ball
Editor: Jon D. Fogdall

Aneko Press Youth

www.anekopress.com

Aneko Press, Life Sentence Publishing, and our logos are trademarks of
Life Sentence Publishing, Inc.
203 E. Birch Street
P.O. Box 652
Abbotsford, WI 54405

JUVENILE FICTION / Religious / Christian / Action & Adventure
Paperback ISBN: 979-8-88936-016-2
eBook ISBN: 979-8-88936-017-9

10   9   8   7   6   5   4   3   2   1
Available where books are sold

CONTENTS

CHAPTER 1

WHERE HAS LINDA GONE?

It was an icy December night in Northern Minnesota. The mercury had struggled up to zero during the day but had dropped out of sight when the sun went down. The wind was increasing in intensity, whipping across the bleak frozen fields, and piling new snow on the drifts of former storms. It was not quite a blizzard that had descended upon Fairview, but it was close.

Fortunately, Danny Orlis had not had to fly that day. He had spent a few hours working on the plane, and the rest of the time answering correspondence. Since it was the regular night for Bible Club, he had gone home at 5 o'clock and was sitting at the kitchen table going over the lesson, when Jim Morgan burst in.

"Hi, Danny!" he exclaimed. "I'm sure glad you're home. It's getting rough outside!"

"I'm glad I'm home tonight, too. Believe me. If I wasn't, I'd be weathered in somewhere for sure."

Danny pushed the Bible aside and glanced at the boy who made his home with them. "Did you clean your boots, Jim?" he asked. "Kay just waxed the floor. She'll have your hide if you track in any snow."

"Don't you worry about my boots. They're as clean as a baby's cheeks." Jim turned a chair around, straddled it, and plumped down, resting his arms on the back. "I'm disappointed that you don't have any more confidence in me than that. You should know me by this time, Danny. I never track in any snow."

"I know you don't," the young pilot replied, "and you know you don't. But that doesn't count for anything. It's Kay who's got to be convinced."

A wide grin twisted Jim's face.

"I'm not afraid of Kay. She's a friend of mine."

"You think she'll be a friend of yours if you track up this kitchen?"

The boy took off his boots and carried them to a burlap sack Kay had placed just inside the door for that purpose.

"What're you doing, Danny?" he asked presently. "Getting ready for tonight?"

"I studied the lesson last night," Danny told him, "but I had a little time, so I thought I'd read through the chapter once or twice before supper."

Jim reached over and took a stalk of celery from the dish on the table.

"S'pose anybody will come tonight?" he asked.

"They should if you did a good job of spreading the news about it."

"I was thinking about the storm. I got the word out, all right. I talked to everyone I could think of. I don't even know how many guys I asked."

"Good boy. I think they'll be here. At least some of them. It takes more than a little snow and cold to stop the kids here." He closed the Bible and pushed back from the table.

"I've really been giving the guys on the basketball team the pitch on Club. I got two definite promises and a couple of maybes." Jim was enthusiastic.

Danny's forehead crinkled and he tugged thoughtfully at the lobe of his ear.

"Do I know them?" he asked.

"You should know them," Jim said. "You saw them both play basketball last year. Matt Dunlap and Joe Cook."

Slowly Danny turned the names over in his mind.

"Matt Dunlap," he said under his breath. "Let's see, he's the big, tall guy who played center."

"That's right. He's six-five and is going to be tops this year." Jim took a long breath and expelled the air slowly. "And there's Joe Cook. He's the fast guy who plays forward."

Danny Orlis nodded. "The skinny one."

"That's him. I talked with both of them two or three times. They both promised they'd come to Club tonight to see what it's like."

"That's great, Jim," Danny said. "Getting guys like those two in Club might help to bring some of the others on the team along."

Neither of them knew that Linda Penner had come into the kitchen until she spoke.

"If you're trying to get Matt Dunlap and Joe Cook out to Club, you'd just as well save your time," she said archly. "They're not square enough to get hooked on Bible Club. I can clue you in on that."

Jim Morgan's frown deepened and, for an instant, anger flared in his eyes.

"Whoever put a nickel in you should get his money back," he retorted. "He got cheated."

She made a face at him and stuck out the tip of her tongue. "Go ahead and ask them to Bible Club and make a fool of yourself. I dare you."

"I already have asked them, and they promised to come."

"They haven't come yet."

"No, but they're going to. They promised."

She shrugged her shoulders indifferently. "If you want to make a fool of yourself, go ahead and ask them again. That's all I've got to say." Her eyes flashed. "I know what they think of you already."

"It doesn't bother me any to make a fool of myself by asking guys to Bible Club," Jim said staunchly. "That's for sure."

Her voice raised. "Well, you *could* think of some of the rest of us who have to live here. The kids at school think we're all a bunch of religious fanatics."

She stomped out of the room before Jim could answer her.

The Morgan boy shook his head. "Sometimes that Linda really burns me up!"

"Don't let it throw you," Danny said. He spoke half in jest, but Jim got the meaning in his voice.

"I still think they'll come," he said, changing the subject. "I've been talking to them about Club for at least a couple of weeks. I don't care what Linda Penner says. I think they're interested. They promised me they'd be here tonight, and I think they will."

A grin spread across the young missionary's face.

"That's the way to go about it, Jim," he said. "Just keep working on the guys out at school and don't get discouraged by disappointments and failures. You'll be surprised at how many will get interested in coming."

Kay Orlis returned from the supermarket then, and it wasn't long until they had supper. Linda Penner sat at the table, tight-lipped and silent, eating only a few bites. Hurt and anger intermingled in her dark eyes.

"Aren't you hungry this evening, Linda?" Kay asked.

"How could I be hungry," she exploded, "when Jim goes around school asking everybody to come to Bible Club until he makes a fool of himself and me and—and all of us a laughingstock?"

Danny Orlis turned to her. "Linda," he said mildly, "Jim hasn't made himself or anyone else a laughingstock."

"That's just what *you* think!"

"Besides, it doesn't matter if people do laugh at us a little because we're witnessing for Christ. That's just one of Satan's tools to keep us from being a testimony for our Lord."

Linda lapsed into silence and, as soon as the others had finished eating, she excused herself and started for her room. The rest of the family sat in the kitchen talking and didn't realize that Linda had left the house until almost time for Club.

Kay turned to her husband.

"Danny, did Linda say anything to you about going out this evening?"

"She certainly didn't. When she left the table, I just figured that she was going to her room to study. Isn't she here?"

"I can't find her anywhere and her coat and hat aren't in her closet." She pursed her lips. "I wonder where she could have gone."

Deliberately Jim Morgan got to his feet.

"Nobody asked me," he announced, "but if you want to know what I think, I figure she slipped out so she wouldn't have to be in on Bible Club this evening. She acts as though it embarrasses her just to have Club meeting here."

The corners of Danny's mouth tightened, and he took a deep breath.

"She *does* act sort of strained whenever Club is mentioned," he answered, "but I don't think you're being entirely fair to Linda, Jim. She never objects to going to the meetings. And when there's a discussion, she takes part as well as anyone else does."

"She may have some very good reason for going out for a little while this evening," Kay said defensively. "She very seldom goes anywhere at night without asking our permission."

Jim Morgan was unconvinced. "Maybe you're right and maybe not. But you just watch. Unless I'm way off she'll come dragging in tonight, just about time for Club to be over, and tell you that she's been to the library or something."

Neither Danny nor Kay Orlis answered him.

"I'm going to have to have a talk with her. She knows better than to leave the house without telling us where she's going and when she'll be back," Danny said.

Kay nodded her agreement.

CHAPTER 2

MATT AND JOE KEEP THEIR WORD

It was Jim Morgan's week to do the dishes. That evening everyone had sat at the table so long visiting, that he got a late start. He was just finishing when the first kids started to arrive for Club. Jim watched the front door anxiously every time the bell rang, but it was not until shortly before 8 o'clock that Matt Dunlap and Joe Cook came.

Jim broke into a wide grin as he saw them and strode purposefully to the front door to greet them.

"Hi, guys!" he exclaimed. "I'm sure glad to see you."

The lanky, dark-haired center glanced around the living room. "We told you that we'd come, didn't we?"

"Sure you did, only–" Jim took their coats into the front bedroom.

"I didn't expect quite so many here," Matt murmured.

"We usually have a real good crowd." Jim turned to the Orlis couple. "Guys, this is Danny and Kay."

Danny shook hands with them warmly. "We're really happy to have you here tonight."

He took them over to chairs beside the place where he had been sitting.

"I watched you both play a lot of basketball last year. When do you have your first game?"

Joe looked at Matt. "In about a week or so, isn't it?"

"I think so. We play Danville."

"Going to have a good team this year?" Danny went on.

The boys grinned modestly. "We should do all right if everybody can stay eligible and we get the breaks."

"I've watched you both. That's quite a hook shot you've got, Joe. I played a lot of basketball when I was in high school and have seen a good many games since, but I don't think I ever saw anyone who does it quite the way you do."

Joe Cook beamed. "That's a little trick I learned from my dad. He used to play college ball for a team down in Iowa."

"It's a mighty valuable trick, if you ask me," Danny replied.

He looked Matt Dunlap over. "Jim was telling me that you've grown a lot in the last year. How tall are you? Six-three?"

The lanky center shook his head. "Six-five-and-a-half," he said.

Danny whistled his amazement. "I'd sure hate to have to try to beat you to getting the ball off the boards. I can tell you that much."

"It helps to be tall," Matt admitted.

Somebody else spoke up just then and the conversation changed. Other kids came straggling into the Orlis living room. Shortly after 8 o'clock the chairs were all filled, and kids were squatting on the floor.

Although they didn't look too comfortable, they sat quietly during the Bible study. It was on a familiar portion of Scripture and the kids entered into the discussion with great spirit. When the meeting was over, the two basketball players, along with Boyd Patterson, Tom Channing, and a couple of other guys, lingered behind asking questions.

"There are some things that came up tonight that I don't understand, Danny," Matt Dunlap said.

"I don't know whether we can answer your questions or not, Matt," Danny answered, "but we can certainly try."

Kay Orlis came to the kitchen door just then.

"How many of you would like to have some hot chocolate and brownies while you talk?" she asked.

Jim Morgan beamed. "You don't even have to *ask* us that, Kay. You already know what the answer is."

"Do you want me to bring them in, or would you like to go out to the kitchen and sit around the table?"

Danny got to his feet.

"I vote for the kitchen. Come on, guys. We'd just as well sit around the table and be comfortable while we talk."

"You don't have to ask me twice to go out into *your* kitchen, Mrs. Orlis," Tom said. "I've been there before."

She smiled graciously.

"Thank you, Tom."

"I only hope you've got a lot of brownies. You're apt to run out tonight."

When they had asked the blessing, Danny turned to Matt Dunlap.

"You said that you had some questions about the Bible study you wanted to ask."

Matt nodded. He returned the cup to the table, a frown clouding his face.

"I don't want to hurt your feelings, Danny," he said, 'but I sure don't get this business of being 'saved' or whatever you call it."

"What bothers you about the term?" Danny Orlis asked him.

"I don't know for sure. It just doesn't make sense to me."

"What would you tell Matt, Jim?" Danny turned to the lad who made his home with him and Kay.

The youthful Christian leaned forward.

"Being 'saved' didn't make sense to me when I first heard it – even when I was going to church and listening to the Bible reading every day. The more I heard the term the madder I got. I figured that I was just as good as anyone else. I didn't need saving.

"That's sort of the way I feel," Matt Dunlap put in.

"It wasn't long though," Jim continued, "until I found out that I wasn't good enough to be saved. I saw that the Bible is right when it says that we are all sinners and are not interested in serving God."

The lanky basketball player bristled slightly. "Now, wait a minute. I've been to church a lot of times. To be frank with you, I go almost every Sunday, and I'm at Sunday school and young people's, too. But at our church the preacher never talks about anything like that. He talks about how we've got to improve the living conditions of the migrant workers and build houses for the people who live in the slums, and see that everyone gets the medical care they need, and things like that. This business of being 'saved' must not be so important or he'd talk about it once in a while."

Joe Cook broke in seriously. "The way I've always figured it is that if I do the best I can and don't harm anyone or break any laws, I'll be all right. Like Matt said just now, if I can help other people, I don't think I'll have to worry when I die. After all, a guy can't do any more than his best."

Danny Orlis nodded.

"The fact that a minister does or doesn't preach about being saved doesn't really mean too much, guys. It's what the Bible says that counts." He breathed deeply. "But you're right about one thing, Joe. A guy can't do any more than his best. The only trouble is that the Bible tells us that our best isn't nearly good enough."

Joe Cook straightened. "I don't think I follow you.

"The Bible says, 'All have sinned and fall short

of the glory of God,' " Danny continued. "There is none righteous, not even one!"

The youthful basketball player grinned and moistened his lips uneasily.

"That's a little hard on a guy, isn't it?" he asked. "Saying all of us have sinned? That doesn't give us much credit for the good we've done." He uncrossed his legs. "I don't know whether I like that or not."

"It isn't a very comfortable thing to think about, I'll admit. But it's true just the same. You see, the Bible says that because God looks down into our hearts. He not only knows all the things we've done in secret or in public. He knows what we've thought – what we've longed to do."

Joe Cook flushed.

"In another place in the Bible," Danny went on, "we're told that 'the wages of sin is death.' So, we have all sinned and have earned death. But God loves us so much that He didn't stop there. 'The free gift of God is eternal life through Jesus Christ our Lord.' "

The two boys were listening intently to every word.

At that very moment, the kitchen door opened, and Linda Penner came bustling in. She stopped suddenly, as she saw who was in the kitchen, and looked from one to another. Color reached up to stain her cheeks.

"Oh–" Her voice choked off suddenly. "Oh I–I thought that everybody would be gone by this time. I mean I thought that Bible Club would be about–"

As she spoke, she realized that her words were only entangling her. Slowly her voice trailed away.

In the awkward silence that followed, Matt Dunlap looked at his watch.

"It's getting late," he said. "We'd better get out of here, Joe, or we'll be late getting in, and the coach will fry us alive."

They got to their feet and moved to the door.

"Thanks a lot for everything."

"You're welcome," Kay said, smiling. "I hope you both will be able to come back to Club next week."

"Oh, we'll be here," Joe Cook said quickly. "There are still some things we want to get straightened out in our minds."

"Any time you have any questions, feel free to call on us," Danny assured them. "We'll be glad to give you any help we can."

When they were finally gone, Linda Penner turned to Danny and Kay Orlis.

"I–I'm sorry I missed Club," she said, her face a livid red. "I–I had to go to the library."

Jim Morgan snickered.

"What'd I tell you, Danny? I knew she'd fool around somewhere until Club was over."

Linda made a face at him and started to stomp from the kitchen.

"Just a minute, Linda," the young missionary said. "I'd like to talk with you before you go to your room."

She came back into the kitchen and stood by the

door. As Danny looked at her, the high color left her face and her thin lips trembled.

"What've I done this time?"

"I think we'd better go into the living room where we can discuss it privately."

"It doesn't bother me to talk in front of Kay and Jim," she countered boldly. "I haven't done anything that I'm ashamed of!"

"That's up to you." Danny spoke quietly but firmly. "You know that we've told you we want to know where and why you go out at night, and when you're going to be in."

Her gaze met his defiantly. "I've told you. I was at the library tonight, studying. And I just got in."

"Linda, you know that you're to let us know before you go, not afterward."

"Daddy never made me account for every minute the way you do. Why, this is worse than being in jail."

"It's a very reasonable request," Danny said.

"I'll do it the next time."

"In order to help you remember, I'm going to ask you to stay home nights for the next week, except to go to church with us."

Anger flashed in her eyes. She glared at him and whirling, stormed into her bedroom and slammed the door.

Jim shook his head.

"What's the matter with her?"

"She's fighting authority, Jim," Kay said. "And it's going to be very hard on her until she realizes that everyone has to obey various regulations."

"And, what's probably more important," Danny put in, "she's fighting God. She's under conviction but won't yield because she wants to rule her own life."

Jim Morgan took a long, deep breath of air, then expelled it thoughtfully.

"If she'd just allow herself to come to the place where she realizes that she can't live her life the way she wants to – that she has to follow either Christ or Satan, she wouldn't keep on fighting God. I know. I found that out before I was saved."

Danny Orlis changed the subject.

"It was certainly good to have Matt and Joe at Bible Club tonight," he said. "They're interested in spiritual things, Jim. And they're willing to listen. You could tell that by talking to them."

The boy nodded. "They sure surprised me. Especially when they said that they went to church regularly. They don't know a thing about the Bible."

Danny Orlis was silent for a moment.

"Unfortunately, there are churches like that. It means that we'll have just that much more difficulty in trying to reach them for the Lord."

He poured himself another cup of hot chocolate.

"If there was just something we could do to get next to them," he said thoughtfully, "something that would help us to make friends with them so that they'd have confidence in us and give us an opportunity to talk to them again."

"If they come to Club again," Kay Orlis said, "you'll be able to get better acquainted with them."

"I've got a better idea than that," Jim Morgan said, grinning.

Danny and Kay both eyed him curiously.

"Now what?"

"I've heard you say a lot of times that the best way you know of to get next to a guy is to take him fishing."

"What's that got to do with it?"

"It's simple," Jim continued. "Take them fishing."

"All right, what're you driving at?" Danny wanted to know.

"Haven't you been reading in the papers lately about how the walleyes are hitting over on Mille Lacs?" Jim Morgan asked. "You and I could take them ice fishing. That would give us a good chance to be good friends with them and talk to them about their souls."

"So that's it!" Kay Orlis exclaimed. "That's a sneaky way to get to go ice fishing, if you ask me."

Danny's eyes lit. "I think you've got a good idea, Jim. A mighty good idea. I've been wanting to get away for a couple of days of ice fishing. I think it would be a wonderful idea to take the boys along."

CHAPTER 3

ICE FISHING PLANS

The following morning at the breakfast table Jim Morgan asked Danny Orlis once more about the ice fishing trip to Mille Lacs. "Did you really mean it, Danny," he asked, "about taking us guys over there ice fishing?"

"Certainly, I did. Haven't you been reading the papers? The ice fishing on Mille Lacs is the best that it's been for years. I've been thinking about getting over there for a couple of days just to try it. Taking the boys along is all the excuse I need."

Jim beamed. "Then I'll talk to the guys this morning. OK?"

"You can find out if they're interested," Danny answered. "If they are, we'll work out a time when they can get away."

"I already can tell you that they're interested – I think."

Jim went to school twenty or thirty minutes early and waited for Joe Cook and Matt Dunlap in the corridor near their home room. When they came in, stomping the snow from their boots, he went over to them.

"Hi, guys."

Their voices were warm and friendly when they replied.

"Hi, Jim," Matt sang out. "What're you doing out here so early in the morning?"

"I've been waiting to talk to you two," Jim replied. "In fact, I've been here for almost half an hour."

Matt Dunlap peeled off his coat and hung it in his locker.

"All I can say is that it must be something mighty important to get you out of bed and over here so early in the morning."

Jim Morgan grinned. "It is mighty important," he said. "Believe me."

A couple of girls came by and spoke to them.

Then Jim asked, "How did you like Club last night?"

Joe Cook picked up his books and turned, quizzically, to his companion.

"It was all right, I guess," he answered. "To tell you the truth, I haven't thought much about it."

But Matt Dunlap broke in quickly. "I thought it was swell, Jim. You know, we talked about a lot of things I'd never heard of until last night. I didn't understand too much about them, but I'd sure like to."

"All you've got to do is keep coming back to Club. Danny can answer any of your questions, and with the Bible, too."

"We just might do that."

They started toward their home room, but Jim stopped them.

"Wait a minute, you guys," he said. "I still haven't told you what I came so early to see you about."

They turned back curiously.

"I just thought you wanted to find out whether we liked Bible Club," Matt answered, "and to see if we were planning on coming back again."

"That was one of the things I wanted to find out," Jim continued "but there's something else." Excitement glittered in his eyes. "How'd you like to do some ice fishing?"

The Dunlap boy shrugged his shoulders indifferently.

"That'd be great if we could go where we could catch something. But there's not much of any place around here."

"I couldn't get very excited about going ice fishing here, myself. But that isn't what Danny and I are planning. How'd you like to go over to Mille Lacs and get in on some real ice fishing?"

Joe Cook's eyes widened, and he caught his breath sharply. "You don't mean that, Jim. You're just kidding."

"Do you think I'd have come over here half an hour early just to kid you? This is the straight goods. I've suggested to Danny that he take some of us guys ice fishing over on Mille Lacs. This time I believe he's going to do it." Jim paused. "If it does work out, how would you like to go along?"

They stared at him as though they could scarcely believe what he was saying.

"That's the way I felt about it. I could hardly wait to talk to you and see if you wanted to go along."

"Want to go along?" Matt echoed. "I've never been ice fishing on Mille Lacs in my life. I won't turn down a chance like that."

"Great. Danny said that I should find out for sure if you'd like to go before he rents a plane from the guy at the airport."

"You mean we'll be flying?" Joe exclaimed incredulously. "You really are kidding now."

"That's what he said. It's just a short flight so it won't cost so much."

The boys still had difficulty in believing Jim.

"Are–are you sure that Danny wants Matt and me to go along?" Joe persisted. "Are you sure that you didn't misunderstand him or something?"

"Of course, if you don't *want* to fly, I'm sure he'd, take the car," Jim Morgan continued.

"Want to fly?" Matt echoed. "Sure we do, don't we, Joe?"

"You can say that again. Maybe you'd better go down and call him right now, Jim, so he'll know for sure that we want to go along." Joe's voice was trembling with excitement. "We don't want him to make arrangements for somebody else to go in our places."

Jim laughed. "You won't have to worry about anything like that happening. Danny said that I should ask you two to go along. That's all the promise we need. He won't ask anyone else until he's found out for sure whether or not you want to go."

"I've never had anything like this happen to me before," Joe said, shaking his head. "I'm afraid the alarm clock will ring and I'll wake up to find out that it's all a dream."

Awed by the prospect of flying over to Mille Lacs with Danny to go ice fishing, Matt and Joe were still talking about it as they went into their home room and Jim Morgan went on down the corridor.

It had worked! They were as excited as he'd ever seen anyone about the chance of going someplace. Danny would have a couple of days with them, so he'd have a good opportunity of getting the conversation around to spiritual things and talking to them about their souls.

And, what's more, they were going to have some wonderful fishing on the best walleye lake in Minnesota. Jim's heart sang.

Jim had a great deal of studying to do during his first library period, but it wasn't easy to keep his mind on it. Not when he kept thinking about all those big Mille Lacs walleyes that they were going to be catching.

* * *

Danny Orlis was as excited about the fishing trip to Mille Lacs as the boys were. He and Jim worked out all their plans and went over them two or three times.

"What we've got to do, Jim," Danny said, "is to get things worked out so we can get away from Fairview just as soon as classes are out at noon."

"Don't worry about that. I'll see that everybody has his gear ready in plenty of time. I'll tell Matt and Joe to get their stuff over here before school Friday morning."

Danny's lips narrowed. "Maybe they'd better bring their stuff over here on Thursday night," he said. "Then I can take it out to the airport when I go out Friday morning."

Listening to them, Kay Orlis laughed pleasantly.

"That's only about the tenth time you two have changed your plans. As excited as you are, a person would think you'd never gone ice fishing before."

"That's what makes it so exciting," her young husband countered. "We know how much fun we're going to have. Don't we, Jim?"

"You and Jim have been talking about using the trip to get better acquainted with Matt and Joe, so you'll have a better chance of winning them for the Lord," Kay said, her eyes twinkling, "but I wonder if that isn't an excuse."

"What do you mean by that?"

"It just sounds to me as though you're more interested in going ice fishing."

Danny Orlis crossed to the sofa and sat down.

"I certainly hope that isn't true," he answered. "I'll admit that fishing is one of the things I enjoy doing as much as anything else, but I've really been wanting to get better acquainted with the boys. They seem to be ripe for the gospel."

The smile fled from Kay's face as she saw that Danny had taken her seriously.

"I didn't mean that," she said. "I was just teasing you."

* * *

During the next few days Matt Dunlap and Joe Cook sought out Jim Morgan at every opportunity to find out the latest word on the trip. They checked with him on the fishing clothes they would need and how much gear each would be able to take along.

"The plane will hold only four of us and our gear," Jim said. "And if we plan on bringing our fish back with us, we'll have to hold the weight down all we can."

Tom Channing and Boyd Patterson happened by just then.

"Fishing?" Boyd echoed. "Who's going fishing?"

"We are," Joe Cook announced. Proudly he told them about the trip they were going to take.

"That sounds great, Jim," Tom put in. "How about it? Is there any chance for us to go along?"

"I doubt it. Danny's renting a plane and it will haul only four of us."

Disappointment gleamed in their eyes.

That evening after supper Tom and Boyd came over to the Orlis home. Danny met them at the door.

"Hi, guys. Come on in."

Boyd Patterson was the spokesman.

"We've only got a minute or two, Danny," he said uneasily, "but there's something that we–we'd like to talk to you about."

"Sure thing." Danny opened the hall closet and took out hangers. "Let me put your coats in here, and we'll go in and sit down."

"Oh, we can't stay that long," Tom put in quickly.

"You're not in that big a hurry," the youthful missionary countered. "Talking goes much better in a nice comfortable chair than it does standing up."

The boys looked at one another, shifting uncomfortably from one foot to the other.

"Do you think we've got time enough for that, Tom?" Boyd asked.

"I have if you have."

"I knew you could be persuaded to stick around," Danny Orlis said. "Who knows? We may even be able to talk Kay into getting out some of those brownies she's been hoarding."

He put their coats away and led them across the living room to the sofa.

"I'm certainly glad you guys came over," Danny began when they were seated comfortably. "What did you think of our Bible study last night?"

"It was great," Tom Channing replied. "We were glad to see so many new guys there."

"So was I – especially Matt and Joe. They acted as though they had real interest in the things of the Lord."

"They're real nice guys, too," Boyd said. "They keep training rules and are always playing for the team. Matt could get bigheaded because he's the star, but he isn't. They're both swell guys."

Danny Orlis nodded. "I'm hoping to get better acquainted with them so I can talk with them about the Lord."

Tom leaned forward slightly. "Is–is that why you're taking them on that ice fishing trip?"

Danny laughed. "Who told you about that?"

"It's all over school," Boyd exclaimed. "Matt and Joe are so excited they're telling everyone about it."

The silence grew heavy.

"The guys have been talking to us about this fishing trip that you're going to take them on, Danny," Boyd put in suddenly. "We–we know that you didn't ask us, and maybe you can't take us, but we sure would like to go along."

"That sounds stupid, doesn't it?" Tom Channing broke in. "We came over here and invited ourselves along on a fishing trip. Come on, Boyd, I think we'd better go home."

"It isn't stupid at all," Danny said quickly. "I'd love to have you guys along, and I know that Jim and Matt and Joe would like to have you, too." He paused momentarily, pulling in a long, deep breath. "The only thing that would be apt to stop it is the fact that we'd sort of planned on flying over there. I thought probably that would be interesting for Matt and Joe." He thought for an instant. "Of course, we could forget about the plane and take the car."

"Oh, don't do that," Tom Channing answered.

"As a matter of fact," Boyd told him, breaking into a grin as he spoke, "it just so happens that we've already thought of that. I've got my car. And since I've started driving the way a Christian guy should drive, Dad will let me go over there, I'm sure. That way you could go ahead and take the other guys in the plane. Tom and I could go in my car."

"That sounds like a great idea to me."

CHAPTER 4

OFF TO MILLE LACS LAKE

Danny Orlis nodded, a broad smile breaking across his face.

"I think that will be a good idea," he said. "You guys can bring most of the gear in the car." He glanced in Jim's direction. "Of course, you want to be sure and have a box – a big box – for all the fish Jim says we're going to catch."

"You can laugh about that, Danny," the boy countered, "but just you wait. I know what the fishing's like over there. You won't be laughing when we start pulling them in."

Tom Channing agreed vigorously. "I've been fishing over on Mille Lacs lots of times and I know what it's like. When you get into a school of those walleyes, you know that you're catching fish. I can tell you that!"

Danny laughed. "We'll see. I've had guys try to sell me on a fishing trip before. They talk big before we go, but they've always got plenty of excuses if things don't turn out the way they say they will."

"We won't need any excuses," Jim said.

Boyd Patterson brought the subject back to the trip they were planning.

"What I want to know is what time do you think we should get away from Fairview Friday?"

The youthful pilot thought for a moment.

"I suppose that depends on what time you can get away, Boyd, but I think you should leave as soon after noon as possible."

"What about us?" Jim asked. "What time are we going to leave? You, I, Matt, and Joe, I mean."

"I think I'll have you guys get excused from classes at two. By the time we get out to the airport and get the plane warmed up, it will be two-thirty. That should get us to the lake at about the same time as Boyd and Tom get there."

The boys were more excited about going ice fishing on Mille Lacs Lake than they had ever been about going fishing anywhere during the summer. They got their sleeping bags and fishing tackle and grub over to Danny and Kay's on Thursday night and, after Bible Club, piled it in the middle of the kitchen floor. Jim Morgan saw Kay looking at it, disapproval on her face.

"Now, Kay," he said, "don't get upset about all that stuff. We'll get it out of here soon enough."

She laughed indulgently. "You'd better get it out of here the first thing in the morning if you expect anything to eat for breakfast. That's all I can say. Why, I can't even get from the refrigerator to the stove."

"Oh, that's easy!" Jim exclaimed. "See." He started to climb over the paraphernalia in the middle of the floor but caught his foot and went sprawling.

"I can see how easy it is. That does it, Jim. If you don't move the gear, you won't get any breakfast in the morning."

"Oh, we'll move it," he said quickly. "We'll move it."

The following morning, while Jim Morgan stood breathlessly beside him, Danny Orlis phoned the airport and got the latest weather information.

"How does it sound?" Jim asked after Danny ended the call.

"Not bad. Not bad at all. Partly cloudy and continued cold."

Kay shook her head in wonderment. "I can see going fishing on a nice warm July day. I even enjoy that myself. But why you would want to leave a nice warm house and go off to a little shack on the ice in the middle of the winter is beyond me."

"To tell you the truth," Danny answered, "I have a hard time making it sound reasonable when I try to explain it to myself."

"I don't," Jim Morgan broke in. "All I have to do is think about those luscious walleyes that are just waiting for us to latch onto them, and I can understand it real easy."

The young pilot nodded. "I guess it isn't too difficult, at that. When you get to school, Jim, be sure to tell Boyd Patterson about the weather forecast."

"That won't affect him and Tom, will it?"

"Only in that they probably won't go if the weather is too bad for us to fly. Why don't you have them stop by here on the way home from school this noon. I'll check on the weather again just before twelve."

Jim went to get his coat.

"I know that I've got to go to school today," he said, "but it's sure going to be tough, I can tell you that much. I'd just as well stay at home. I know I won't be learning anything."

At the front door he glanced back over his shoulder. "I sure hope the fish are biting."

Danny Orlis laughed good-naturedly. "From the way I get it, there's not much question about that, is there? According to what you told me, we're going to have trouble getting our hooks in the water before the fish hit them."

Jim colored delicately. "I think fishing's going to be good. It usually is. But you've been fishing lots of times. You know how that goes."

"Don't go to alibiing already. You're the one who talked us into this trip. You'd just better produce, that's all I can say. If you don't, you're really going to be in trouble."

The weather forecast was still the same when Danny checked at noon. Tom and Boyd left Fairview at the time they had planned. And at 2 o'clock Danny and Kay picked up Jim and his friends at school and drove out to the airport. Matt Dunlap glanced up at the dull gray clouds that were drifting aimlessly across the sky.

"How about it, Danny?" he asked. "Do the fish bite when the weather's like this?"

"You'll have to ask Jim," Danny said, jerking his head in the Morgan boy's direction. "This is his trip. He's the authority. Or didn't you know?"

"Now, wait a minute, Danny!" A protest glinted in Jim's eyes. "You've done a lot more ice fishing than I've ever done. You know when the fish bite and when they don't."

Danny winked at his companions.

"But you're the one who picked Mille Lacs Lake. And, believe me, if we don't get our limits of five-pound walleyes, we know just whom to blame."

Jim Morgan squirmed. "I know the fish are there," he said lamely, "and a lot of other people go there and catch them. But I can't say for sure whether we're going to get any."

"Don't try to get out of it," Joe said.

The flight over to Mille Lacs Lake was beautiful. The wind had come up briefly at midmorning, but now it had died to a whisper. The sun peeked through the clouds to glint brightly on the snow-flocked forest.

It was a short flight, and almost before the boys realized they were close, Danny Orlis was circling the lake in front of Garrison. Jim was the first to spot Boyd Patterson's car.

"Danny!" he cried. "There they are!"

The young pilot banked and came about. Boyd Patterson and Tom Channing had spotted them as they had flown over the first time. They were standing together on the ice, between their car and the fish house. Danny dipped a wing in greeting, and the boys below waved frantically.

"That's them, all right," Danny said, "but I'm afraid we're not going to be able to land too close to them."

"Why not?" Jim wanted to know.

"The ice looks awfully rough near our fish house." Matt Dunlap looked out across the lake.

"There sure aren't very many fishermen out today," he said. "I thought the lake would be full."

"People probably have gotten tired of all this fishing and no fish," Danny said, "so they've packed up their gear and have gone home."

"Take it easy, will you, Danny? You talk that way, but you know as well as I do that Mille Lacs is a good walleye lake. It's one of the best in the entire state."

"The time for talk is past, Jim. Now you've got to start proving up on all these fish promises you've been making to us."

Danny brought the plane in to a perfect landing on the frozen lake and taxied as close as he could to the fish house. The prop had scarcely stopped turning before his passengers piled out.

Tom and Boyd ran to meet them.

"Hi! Where've you been? We thought you would never get here."

"We got worried about all those big fish we were going to catch and had to go back for some stronger hooks and fines," Joe said, joking.

Matt and Joe got their cameras out of the plane while Jim turned to the two guys who had come by car.

"Caught any fish yet?" he asked.

"Caught any fish?" Tom echoed. 'We're not that fast. We just got our minnows and got out here. We haven't even had time to get the car unpacked yet."

"Well, I'm glad you didn't get started fishing," Jim replied. "Even if you had caught some, Danny wouldn't have believed it. He'd have accused you of buying them somewhere in order to make me and the lake look good."

Danny had been joking with the guys all the way over from Fairview, but now he was serious as he worked at the plane.

"If you guys want to help me get the aircraft tied down, we can get to fishing that much sooner," he said.

All five of them hurried to him.

"Just tell us what you want us to do, Danny," Joe said, "and we'll do it."

"We're going to have to stake the aircraft down so the wind won't blow it away." Danny showed them how to drive pins into the ice to anchor the plane.

Once they finished, he double-checked their work, secured the ties, and snubbed them taut. At last he was satisfied. "There. That should hold it."

"You don't expect the little wind that's blowing now to take the plane away, do you?"

Danny shook his head. "No, I don't. But, you know, we must always be ready and prepared for any emergency. If the wind does come up, it's going to be too late to tie down the plane." He took a deep breath. "Remember this, guys, whether you fly yourself or with someone else. Insist that every precaution be taken at all times. It doesn't take many brains for a pilot to be foolhardy and take chances. The smart pilot is careful enough so that he never has to find out just how brave he is."

Jim Morgan picked up the ice auger and started toward the fish house.

"Let's get the holes cut so we can prove to Danny that there really are walleyes here."

"You don't mean to tell me that little auger is going to make a hole big enough to let us take *these* walleyes, is it?" Danny glanced at Tom Channing and winked broadly.

CHAPTER 5

AT THE MERCY OF THE STORM

While the other guys were getting the gear out of the car and plane, and stashing it away in the fish house, Jim Morgan set to work with the auger, cutting through the ice in the floorless half of the building.

"I can't understand why these holes weren't cut and the fire started so our fish house would be warm," Danny said, looking up from the little airtight heater where he was building a wood fire. "I thought, from the information we had from the resort owner, that the holes would be cut and the fire going."

"Maybe they don't know we're here," Jim Morgan said.

"They should know. Boyd and Tom stopped for minnows before they came out here."

"Oh well, this isn't so bad," Jim said, leaning on the auger momentarily. "Whenever I get to thinking what hard work it is to cut these holes, I think about all those fish we're going to catch, and that soon wakes me up."

"Now who's talking about fish?"

"You guys have convinced me that I know all there is to know about fishing. You've made me realize that I'm an expert."

By the time Jim had finished cutting six holes in the ice, the other boys had finished their tasks and were busy rigging up their fishing rods.

Matt Dunlap took a minnow from one of the buckets and held it in his bare hand. "How do you hook the minnow for this kind of fishing, Danny?"

"Just behind the dorsal fin – the same way you would hook a minnow for still fishing in the summertime."

Matt did as he was directed.

"Use a bobber?"

"No, you won't have any use for a bobber. Just put enough weight on to take your line down. Let it go down to the bottom and raise it up six inches or so – to the place where it's floating free the way a minnow would be apt to swim."

Tom Channing caught a minnow and was busy following Danny's instructions.

"That's the same way I hook minnows when I fish for walleyes in–" He didn't get to finish what he was saying. "I've got one!" he cried exultantly. "I've got one!"

A moment later he pulled a fat, struggling walleye from the water and held him up admiringly.

"Just look at that," he said, pride edging his voice. "Just look at that for a fish, now, would you?"

Jim Morgan laughed. "Take a look at what Tom's holding, Danny! Take a good, long look. That happens to be a walleye, in case you didn't know."

"That's right. Rub it in. And after I brought you all the way out here."

"I just wanted you to appreciate what you're getting, that's all. What did I tell you about the walleye fishing on Mille Lacs? Didn't I say it was as good as it is back home on the Angle?"

Danny Orlis chuckled good-naturedly. "You wouldn't do all that crowing over one poor ignorant little fish, now, would you? Back home we don't even use that kind for bait."

"I'll bet you'd use it for bait if you caught one like it. You can talk all you want to. That doesn't change the way things are. We've only been fishing for a minute or two and already we've got a fish. I wouldn't be a bit surprised if some of us would get our limits tonight."

"Oh, now, come off it. We've been fortunate, I'll admit, but we're not going to catch our limits tonight. We'll be doing well if we get anything else."

Joe Cook squealed excitedly. "Don't be so sure about that, Danny! I tell you, I've got a whopper!'"

Danny Orlis reached for his rod and reel.

"That does it!" he muttered, baiting his hook. "It's time to stop talking and get to fishing."

Fishing was good that evening, better than even Jim Morgan could possibly have hoped for. In a couple of hours they had caught several more average-sized walleyes. Darkness had settled in for the night and they had lit the lantern on the table. Finally, Danny quit fishing and went over to the stove.

"All right, you guys," he said, "which one of you is going to help me fix us something to eat?"

Jim Morgan reeled in his line and got to his feet.

"I'll fillet those fish you thought we weren't going to catch, Danny," he said good-naturedly. "That is, if you can bring yourself to fry them."

The young pilot glanced at their companions and winked.

"I can fry them all right. Don't you worry about that. But do you think we dare to eat them, Jim?"

"Just what do you mean by that? There just aren't any better fish for eating than walleyes, and especially when they come from Mille Lacs Lake."

"Oh, I know that, but I thought you would want to be sure and have some fish to take home. We might not get any more, you know."

Jim laughed. "You can talk, but you know better than that. We've only been fishing a little while and look what we've got already. We're going to get all the fish we need for eating and still have plenty to take home."

Danny Orlis stepped outside to get an armload of wood from the pile at the corner of the fish house. For a brief instant he remained motionless, testing the wind with his face. It was getting colder now, and the wind was beginning to come up. Stars still winked brightly in the darkness overhead, but the western horizon was dark and forbidding. There could just be a storm in the offing. He got an armload of wood and went back inside.

It was several minutes later when he turned to Matt Dunlap. "You brought that radio of yours along, didn't you, Matt?"

"I sure did. I never go anywhere without it."

"Have you tried it since we got here?"

The lanky basketball player shook his head.

"Nope. I've been so busy fishing, I haven't had time. What's the matter, Danny? Want to get a little rock 'n roll?"

"Hardly. I want to get the weather forecast. Why don't you turn it on?"

Matt got his radio and turned it on to one of the Minneapolis stations. The announcer's voice was so faint Danny could scarcely hear him.

"Can't you turn it up any louder than that?"

"The volume's way up. Guess maybe my batteries are about shot. I knew I should've gotten some when I was downtown yesterday morning, but this trip sort of ran me short on dough."

"The batteries will be strong enough to get what we want," Danny said. "If they're not, I can go over and try to get the weather on the plane radio."

In a few minutes, the weather forecast came on.

Matt pressed his ear close to the radio speaker and tried to catch the words.

"Pipe down, you guys!" he sang out. "I can't hear a thing!"

Everything quieted save for the crackling of the little wood heater.

"You aren't expecting a storm, are you, Danny?" Joe Cook asked uneasily after a moment or two.

"Not exactly. I just wanted to find out what the forecast is."

"It doesn't sound too bad," Matt announced after two or three minutes. "We're supposed to have a few snow flurries and a little lower temperature tonight, with a low of 18 below. There's not supposed to be much temperature change tomorrow."

Danny Orlis nodded but said nothing. For a time, he stared across the little room, then went to the door and looked out. Jim Morgan saw what he was doing and came over beside him.

"What're you looking for, Danny?" he asked.

"I don't know. Nothing, I guess."

Danny glanced in Matt's direction. "Are you sure you got that weather report right?"

"Sure I did. I repeated it to you just the way the announcer gave it. Why?"

"I suppose I'm being unduly concerned," Danny went on, "but I just don't like the feel of the air tonight. I'm afraid we're going to have a change in the weather."

Boyd Patterson laughed. "My grandma used to be able to feel a storm coming," he said. "Or at least she said she could. She claimed she could tell by the way her rheumatism started to act up. Is that the way you know, Danny?"

"A fine bunch of guys you are," the young pilot grumbled good-naturedly. "Here I take you on a trip like this, and you won't even listen to me when I try to tell you that I think there's a storm coming."

"That's all right, Danny. If you want to think a storm is on the way, we won't say a word," Matt Dunlap put in. "To tell you the truth, if the fishing would stay like this, I wouldn't mind being stranded out here for about a week."

Danny went back to his cooking. "You guys can kid about it if you want to, but the air does feel funny tonight – almost exactly the way it does when a bad storm is on the way." He turned the fish in the frying pan and salted them. "Then, too, we're about the only ones on the lake tonight. That seems strange to me, too."

"But we heard the forecast," Matt said. "And it wasn't anything to frighten anyone."

"I don't think it means anything that the fishermen aren't here yet," Jim Morgan put in. "From what I've heard, most of the guys who come here to fish come from St. Cloud and the Twin Cities. They probably don't get off from work in time to get up here on Friday night. Just wait until tomorrow. I'll bet that every fish house on the lake will be filled.

At least they will be if the people have heard of the way the fish are biting."

On the hour Danny Orlis had Matt turn on his radio again.

"I'd just like to find out what the new forecast is," he said, trying to keep the concern from his voice.

"OK." Matt switched on his radio and listened intently.

"What's the matter?"

"Sorry, Danny, but there's nothing. Nothing at all. The batteries are gone."

Danny stood there momentarily, staring at the little stove. Then he turned and went over to the corner where his parka hung.

"Where're you going, Danny?" Jim Morgan asked.

"I suppose it's foolish, but I'll feel a little better if I have the weather forecast. Thought I'd go over to the plane and see if I can pick up anything."

"Boy, supper's all ready, and we're plenty hungry. Can't you wait until we eat?"

"You guys go ahead. I can eat when I get back."

Jim Morgan got his parka and slipped it on. "I'll go with you."

The young pilot started to protest but checked himself. "Good."

Together they went out into the frigid night air and walked briskly toward the plane.

"Do you really think it's going to storm, Danny?" Jim asked.

"I don't know. I certainly hope not." They walked half a dozen paces or so. "But if it does, I sure don't want to be caught out here on the lake."

Jim looked about uneasily. The darkness seemed to be closing in about them.

"It's getting a little colder, I think," he said. "And the wind seems to be coming up, but I don't think it's going to storm."

"Maybe, and maybe not."

"I sure hope it isn't, anyway," the boy continued. "The fishing's going to be great tomorrow. I can feel it in my bones."

At the plane Danny switched on the radio and listened intently.

"Won't the plane radio come in any better than that?" Jim asked presently.

"Not on the ground. In fact, it's not often that a plane radio will pick up a signal more than forty or fifty miles away when on the ground."

But fortunately, the radio did pick up the station in Brainard.

"Severe weather warnings," the announcer droned. "I repeat. Severe weather warnings. Snow and high winds from the Canadian border to the Iowa line beginning at about 11 o'clock tonight in the Detroit Lakes and Bemidji areas and spreading across the entire state and into Wisconsin by daylight tomorrow morning."

The young pilot frowned as he switched off the radio and turned to his companion.

"That doesn't sound so good, Jim."

"But I–I thought Matt's forecast called for light snow."

"The report Matt got did sound all right, but the signal was so weak it wasn't possible for him to hear well enough even to know what station he was listening to, or what section that weather forecast was for. But this was the straight goods. It came from the weather station in Minneapolis. There's no doubt about its being true."

Jim Morgan's thin face paled, and for a moment fright stole into Iris' voice.

"Wh-wh-what are we going to do now, Danny?"

"We're going to get out of here just as quickly as we can." Danny's hands went mechanically to the plane controls. "Go and tell Boyd to get his car started and get you guys back to Garrison just as fast as he can."

"What about you?"

"I'll taxi the plane over there."

"OK. We'll get to Garrison and wait for you there." Jim started for the fish house on the run.

"On the double!" Danny called out after him. "And move the rest of those guys along. There's no time to lose."

Once Jim was gone and Danny was alone, he tried the starter. The engine groaned in protest, but there was no responding roar. His heart skipped a beat. What if it wouldn't start?

He had diluted the oil with gas when they landed. He recalled that distinctly. And the battery had been up good before they left Fairview. Still the starter wouldn't turn the engine over.

Concern tugged at his heart as he got out and, grasping the propeller with both hands, swung it sharply.

There was no response.

He tried again, and again.

It didn't seem cold enough to keep the engine from starting, he reasoned, but that was the only thing that could be wrong. The airport mechanic had checked the engine out thoroughly that very morning, and he had double-checked it himself to be sure that everything was in first-class condition. There was no reason why the plane wouldn't start.

Determinedly he forced such thoughts from his mind. There was no time to worry about why the plane wouldn't start. He had to get it going, and right away.

It was a good thing he had the firepot and engine tent along. At least he had what he needed to get the engine going again – if being cold was all that was wrong with it. All it would do would be to delay him for an hour.

He looked anxiously up at the sky. The clouds had all but blotted out the stars. The storm was building fast. It wouldn't be long until new snow would be falling.

Did he have an hour?

Hurriedly Danny rummaged in the back of the plane for the canvas engine tent. He had not yet found it when a sharp explosion sounded above the wind. Danny Orlis froze. His breath choked off and fear tightened its fingers about his throat.

He knew, all too well, the meaning of that sound. It slammed barbed darts deep into his heart. The ice on big bodies of water like Mille Lacs Lake didn't always lie dormant from freeze-up to breakup. It heaved and cracked unexplainably, especially when the weather was the coldest, to throw up long jagged furrows or open into treacherous, black water leads.

Danny crawled out of the plane and dropped to the ice. In the minute or two he had been in the little cabin, the snow had begun to swirl over the frozen lake in great, choking clouds. It drove through his clothes and snatched the breath from his lungs.

The boys! He had to get to them!

Grimly, Danny left the plane and staggered toward the fish house. If a lead should open between him and the place where the boys were waiting, he would never be able to see it until he fell – until he – He dared not even think about it!

Danny slowed uncertainly. The snow had blotted out the light that marked the location of the fish house!

CHAPTER 6

ANXIOUS INTERLUDE

Back in the fish house Matt Dunlap turned anxiously to Jim Morgan, whose eyes were dark with fear.

"Are you guys ready?" Jim demanded.

"Just a second! We want to get our fish!"

"OK, but let's get a move on! I don't like the looks of this."

Joe snatched up the string of fish and started for the door.

The wind blasted across the open ice, sweeping the snow in great, swirling clouds. Boyd Patterson stared uneasily into the darkness.

"What do you think, Boyd?" Jim asked uneasily. "Can we make it?"

"I think so," he said with a confidence that was not in his heart. "But it's not going to be easy. I can tell you that much."

The boys piled into the car, and Boyd turned the key. The engine groaned in protest as it turned over.

"It's got to start," Jim said under his breath. "It's just got to start!"

Boyd tried again. The engine sputtered and caught with a gratifying roar.

He wiped the sweat from his forehead with a trembling hand. "For a minute there, I didn't think it was going to start!"

"I was sure praying," Jim Morgan said thankfully.

For a short space of time, they sat in the car waiting for the engine to warm up. Each passing minute seemed to send the snow whirling higher about the car. Jim saw how the snow was drifting and turned to Boyd.

"Think you can follow that road on the ice so we'll be sure and get to Garrison?"

"They had it planned well enough so anyone could follow it," Boyd said. Then he added uncertainly, "If it doesn't drift shut, and we can see."

"Has anyone heard Danny go by yet?" Joe Cook wanted to know.

"I haven't," Jim answered. "Maybe he had as much trouble getting his engine started as we did."

"Or he might have gone, and we missed him."

"You don't think he'd go off and leave us, do you?" Joe persisted.

"Not Danny." Jim Morgan was emphatic. "He said for us to go on and meet him in Garrison, but I know him well enough to know that he wouldn't go on himself until he was sure that we got away all right."

There was a short silence.

For answer Boyd flipped the gearshift lever to low and depressed the accelerator. The wheels spun.

"Wh-wh-what's the matter?" Matt Dunlap demanded, fear thick in his voice.

Boyd tried again, but the car didn't move.

"Come on, you guys!" Jim jumped out of the car.

"Let's get to shoving! We've got to get going."

The wind drove through their heavy parkas as they pushed at the stalled car. Boyd raced the engine, but it was no use.

"We're stuck, but good!" Boyd admitted at last.

Joe Cook reached in the open car door and grasped him by the arm. "Wh-what are we going to do?"

"I think we'd just as well go back into the fish house. There's nothing we can do staying out here."

They got their sleeping bags and trooped back into the fish house.

"What about Danny?" Matt asked. "Do you think he could taxi in this wind and snow even if he did get the engine started?"

Jim Morgan shook his head. "I don't see how he could. He'll be back."

"If he were coming, he'd be back by now." Joe Cook went to the door and stared out into the howling storm. "I think he's gone on and left us."

"Oh, no, he hasn't," Jim Morgan repeated, choking

down his own concern. "Maybe he had to do something to the plane before he could come back. Maybe one of the ties came loose or something. He–he'll be along in a minute or two."

"Well, I'm not staying here any longer without going to find out for sure what's happened to Danny," Boyd Patterson exclaimed. As he spoke, he was buttoning his parka. "I'm like you, Jim. I know Danny. And I know he wouldn't leave us this way without a good reason. He's had plenty of time to put down two or three new ties and then some, and still get back here."

"That's what I've been thinking," Joe exclaimed, his voice quavering. "And what's going to happen to us if he doesn't come back?"

"I'm a lot more interested in what's happened to Danny right now," Boyd said firmly. "It isn't so far over to the plane. I'm going over and see what's happened to him." He pulled on his mittens and started out the door. "Danny could have gotten hurt trying to work with the plane alone. That's what I'm afraid of."

Jim Morgan grasped Boyd by the arm, resisting his efforts to pull away.

"Now, wait a minute, Boyd. We've got to use our heads."

"That's just what I'm doing. We've got to get over there and see what's happened to Danny before he freezes or something."

"I'm just as concerned about Danny as you guys," Jim went on, "but we've got to be smart about what we do. We wouldn't have a chance of finding the plane at night, as hard as it's snowing right now. I don't think we could find it if it was still daylight, and the plane wasn't more than half a block away. Just look out there at the way the snow's blowing. We can't even see the car."

The Patterson boy turned to face him, anguish and anger mingling in his eyes.

"You can do what you want to, Jim Morgan. I'm going out and look for Danny. I'm not going to let him lie out there and–and freeze to death!"

"Oh, no, you're not!" Jim's voice raised authoritatively. "You're going to stay here with the rest of us.

"Who's going to make me?"

Jim's voice lowered. "I know just exactly how you feel. And don't think I don't want to go out and try to find him. Danny is just like a–a dad to me."

"Then what're we standing here for? That storm isn't getting any better."

"One of the things Uncle Carl Orlis used to tell us so often back home at the Angle was that if one person was lost in a bad storm, the others shouldn't go out and try to find him until the storm let up. He said that going out that way is almost a positive way of getting somebody else lost or hurt trying to find the other person." Jim ran a trembling hand across his face. "I–I'd like to go out right now and try to find out what has happened to him, but I know it's not the thing to do. Danny's a real woodsman. He knows how to take care of himself out in a storm like this a lot better than we would."

"But if he's hurt," Matt put in, "he wouldn't be able to take care of himself."

"That's just it. We don't know if he's hurt or not. We don't know whether he decided to hole up in the plane for a while, or whether he missed the fish house, or–" His voice trailed away.

The sharp report echoed over the noise of the wind.

"What was that?" Joe Cook asked fearfully.

Jim tried to ignore him. "The best thing we can do is to build up the fire and wait right here for Danny. He'll be along. I'm sure he will."

"What was that noise?" Joe demanded.

"What noise?"

"You heard it the same as I did. It–it sounded like someone had set off a charge of dynamite."

"Or the cracking of the ice," Tom Channing put in. "I've heard that noise lots of times."

"You–you mean the ice is beginning to crack up?" Joe Cook asked.

"It might mean that, and it might not," Jim said, trying to sound unconcerned. But that was not easy. Especially when he realized all too well that there could be dangerous stretches of open water across the ice, stretches the unwary traveler might very well stumble into.

Tom Channing whirled to face Jim, frustration and anger clouding his eyes.

"If we're not going out to look for Danny," he said bitterly, "what are we going to do? We can't just sit here and—and let him freeze to death without even trying to help him."

Jim thought for a moment. What if they were right, he asked himself. What if Danny had broken a leg or hurt himself so he couldn't go on alone, and was lying out on the ice in the sub-zero weather, freezing to death? Could he ever forgive himself if he kept the guys from going out to look for Danny, and—and Danny froze to death?

Grimly he pushed such thoughts aside. He had heard often enough what to do in a situation like this. Now, the thing was to have courage enough to do it.

"Oh, God," he prayed inwardly, "just help me to have the courage to do what I know we should do!"

"First off," he said aloud, "we're going to get that lantern out where Danny will be able to see it in case he does try to find us in this storm. Then we'd better get that pile of wood inside. We don't know for sure how long this storm's going to last. We've got to have plenty of wood to burn."

It seemed strange to Jim, but the other boys seemed to accept his leadership. Tom Channing already had the lantern and took two or three steps toward the door. Then he turned back, got a piece of strong casting line, and went out to tie the lantern securely to the corner of the building, where Danny would be the most apt to see it if he was stumbling toward them in the snow. Tom was only gone a minute or two, but the wind had driven the snow into the folds of his parka so that he was chilled through and panting breathlessly.

The other guys followed Tom Channing's lead, got into their heavy coats, and began to lug the pile of wood into the fish house, armload by armload. The cold clawed and tore at them, and the snow found every tiny crevice in their clothes. Yet they did not stop until the last stick of wood was in the fish house. Once that was accomplished, they sank, exhausted, to the floor, where they lay, breathing heavily.

"I'm glad that's done." Jim said wearily, "I thought we were going to freeze to death."

"I can see now why you didn't want to go out and try to find Danny," Matt Dunlap said. "I don't believe we'd have lasted a hundred yards."

"And if we had, we couldn't have found our way back." At the thought of Danny, fear gleamed in Jim's eyes. "I know we did what was best, even though it is awfully hard to stay here when we know what could be happening to Danny."

No one else said anything.

After a time, Tom Channing got to his feet and checked the fire in the airtight heater.

"We'd better take it as easy as we can with our wood," Jim cautioned. "We don't know how long it's going to have to last."

Tom returned one stick to the pile and sat down

in a chair. For several minutes he held his hands out to the stove, warming them.

Nobody said much, although they all looked at their watches every now and then. As the time passed, Matt Dunlap's frown deepened.

"You know, guys, there are some things I don't understand about this Christian business."

"Like what?" Boyd Patterson wanted to know.

"Like what's happened to Danny. He's such a good guy. He could've brought some other men along on this fishing trip, but he didn't. He just brought us. And now he's out in this storm somewhere and–and nobody knows what's happened to him. Why would God let this happen?"

Joe Cook leaned forward intently. In the semi-darkness they could just make out the growing fear in his angular face.

"I've been wondering about the same thing." Joe took a deep breath and expelled it in a long, thin stream. "Danny likes to fish and all that, but I had the hunch that he only came on this trip because we wanted to come so bad. Or at least that's the way I've got it figured."

"He's a missionary, too," Matt continued. "I don't know for sure what a missionary does, but I guess he spends his whole life helping other people." He got to his feet and walked nervously over to the door and back again. "Why did it happen that he's the one who is lost? Doesn't God care about him?"

Jim Morgan answered.

"Of course God cares about Danny. He cares about all of us. But, you know, a lot of people seem to have that sort of an idea about what it is to be a Christian. They seem to think that all anyone has to do is to accept Christ as his personal Savior and he'll never have any more problems or troubles. That isn't true at all."

"That's exactly right," Boyd Patterson put in. "I know a lot of people who seemed to have more troubles after they took Christ as their Redeemer than they did before. God promises to give us the strength and courage to take what comes. He doesn't promise to make everything easy for the one who believes in Him."

Joe took a long, deep breath. "It just doesn't seem fair to me."

Tom Channing cleared his throat. "I know it seems as though God doesn't care for the believer when He doesn't prevent every problem from coming up. But there's another way to look at it. When we put our trust in Christ to save us, He does just that. If anything should happen to Danny or anyone else who is a Christian, God will take him home to be with Him. His future is sure." Tom paused significantly. "If a person who isn't a Christian dies, he's lost forever. So, you see, in the thing that really counts, God does take care of the one who has been born again."

Joe Cook coughed and swallowed nervously. "I'd never thought of it that way before," he managed.

Nobody spoke for several minutes. The only sound was the roar of the wind and the crackling of the wood fire in the stove. The fishing tackle and minnows were forgotten in the far corner of the fish house.

After a time, Jim Morgan straightened suddenly and turned his head from one side to the other.

"What's the matter?" Tom Channing demanded.

"Did–did you guys hear something?" Jim wanted to know.

Silence gripped them.

"Did you?" Matt put in.

"I thought I did," Jim went on, "but now I'm not so sure. Maybe I–I didn't hear anything after all."

He got up and went over to the door and opened it. A blast of frigid air slapped him in the face. He stared numbly out into the emptiness of the night. There was nothing he or anyone else could do to help Danny Orlis. Absolutely nothing. That realization swept over him like an icy cloud.

Numbly he closed the door and turned back to the other guys.

"You know," he said, his voice quivering in spite of himself, "there's something we haven't done yet. We haven't prayed about this."

"I've been praying for Danny ever since we got back here and he didn't come," Tom Channing said.

"So have I," Boyd put in.

"I've been praying to myself, too. But we need to pray together."

"Prayer!" Joe Cook snorted miserably. "What good's it going to do to pray? That isn't going to help Danny find us any sooner."

"It can," Jim replied confidently, "and it can keep Danny safe from harm until somebody does find him." He took his Testament and turned to chapter 14 of John's Gospel.

"My faith usually needs to be strengthened when there's something important to pray about," he said. With that he started to read. " 'Truly, truly, I say to you, he who believes in Me, the works that I do, he will do also; and greater works than these he will do; because I go to the Father. Whatever you ask in My name, that will I do, so that the Father may be glorified in the Son. If you ask Me anything in My name, I will do it.' "

When Jim finished reading, they all knelt on the floor of the fish house and began to pray. Matt Dunlap and Joe Cook eyed one another uncertainly, but did as the others did, except that they did not take their turns in praying.

CHAPTER 7

"NOBODY KNOWS WE'RE STRANDED"

The storm continued to build in intensity. The wind roared across the frozen lake, driving the snow, like sand in a desert storm, before it. The snow bit savagely into Danny Orlis' raw, frost-chilled face. He staggered forward over the rough ice. The howling wind drove against him with the force of a battering ram, hammering the breath back into his lungs until he had to turn his head and fight to breathe.

The cold pierced his heavy clothing with numbing intensity that seemed to build from one moment to another. It stole the strength from his legs and seemed to hang weights on each muscle in his body.

He caught his toe on a piece of rough ice and sprawled forward, arms outstretched, into a huge drift. The snow was shoved inside the sleeves of his parka. And it burned his face. For a brief space of time, he lay there without the strength to move. It would be so easy, so very easy, to lie there and let the snow cover him. He was so weary–so very weary.

But he couldn't lie there that way when the boys might be needing him this very minute! Whatever else happened, he had to get to them. Grimly he stirred himself. He had to force himself to his feet. He had to go on!

Danny drew up one leg and then the other. Momentarily he crouched on all fours before he could force himself upright once more. Grimly he pushed forward, unmindful of the snow and darkness that made a swirling, choking, opaque curtain that swallowed him completely and blotted out his vision and all sense of direction.

Danny staggered forward into the teeth of the wind. After a few steps, his reason returned.

He had started in the right direction from the plane for the fish house. He was sure of that. But something must be wrong, or he'd have reached the boys by this time. He had already been out on the ice for a far longer time than it should have taken for him to cover the distance between the plane and the fish house.

Realization of that fact came slowly but come it did. And with it a numbing sensation akin to paralysis. There was only one explanation! And the very thought chilled him inwardly as the snow and cold could never do!

Very clearly, he saw what had happened. He had passed the fish house in the storm. He was lost. LOST!

Danny Orlis checked his forward motion and, almost mechanically, turned his back against the fierce anger of the storm. For the space of a minute or two he stood there without moving. He breathed with great difficulty, forcing the frigid air into his burning lungs.

The wind was blowing so strongly it was all Danny could do to keep from moving along with it. In fact, he took a staggering step or two before he was able to force himself to stop.

"Dear God!" he prayed in anguish between clenched teeth, "You know I'm in a real mess tonight. I'm lost out here on the lake and the boys are in the fish house, wherever it is. Please God, keep them inside where they're safe and–and keep them from trying to–to come out after me. And, if it's Your will, just help me to find the fish house."

Danny Orlis' first impulse was to run blindly, first in one direction and then another, in a frantic effort to find his way. He had felt that same way on other occasions when he had been lost. But that was no good. Dad Orlis had warned him a thousand times.

"The man doesn't live who won't get lost in the woods or in a storm," he had said so often. "It's what he does after he realizes that he's lost that tells whether he's a real woodsman or not. So, when you get lost, Danny, stop right where you are and think. Think! That's why God gave you a mind."

Danny made himself stand stock still while he reviewed the situation carefully. When he crawled out of the plane after making his decision to go back to the fish house the wind had been quartering in from the northwest. That was substantially the same direction he had to go to reach the boys.

He wouldn't have gone west of the fish house. He was quite sure of that. The natural tendency would have been to drift slightly with the wind, in spite of his best efforts to keep going in a straight line.

There was only one thing for him to do. He had to get oriented – get to the plane or the road the resort owner had plowed out on the ice, or even another fish house. Anything to help him learn exactly where he was. Then he would be able to do something about finding the boys.

His best chance was to try to locate the aircraft. He turned deliberately and began to follow his own footsteps back through the drifts. The wind and blowing snow were filling them rapidly, but he had stumbled and fallen often enough to mark the path well. He made his way back, one step at a time. Every few feet he stopped and stared intently into the darkness, hoping against hope that he might get a glimpse of Boyd's car, the fish house, or the plane – anything that would tell him where he was.

A prayer welled constantly in his aching heart.

He lost all track of time. He was alone in a sea of snow – as alone as though he were the only person in the world, enveloped in a billowing white cloud that blinded his vision, drove the cold to the very sinews of his powerful young body, and choked his lungs.

Bands of steel tightened on his chest until his lungs were set aflame, and his legs throbbed with exhaustion. Every fiber of his being cried out for rest. Still, he could not stop, nor could he turn back. He had to go on. On! On! He had to reach the boys before they did something rash and foolish!

Doggedly Danny drove onward, step by step. Through a drift waist deep he lunged, and over a jagged ridge of ice. He stopped suddenly! That ridge of ice was familiar! It had been the thing that caused him to land some distance from the fish house in the first place. All he had to do was turn and follow it west, and he would find the row of fish houses.

Why hadn't he thought of that when he crossed it the first time?

The realization that he had found something tangible sent new strength coursing through his tired body. The drifts were as deep as ever. The storm was just as furious as it had been a few moments before. But they didn't seem as bad. Danny quickened his pace.

He followed the ridge of ice a hundred yards or so almost due west before coming to the high banks of snow, now almost hidden by new drifts, that marked the road the resort had plowed out to the fish houses.

That meant–. Briefly he stopped and stared hard into the whirling snow and darkness. There was a fish house not more than thirty feet away!

"Thank You, God!" he breathed prayerfully. "Thank You!"

He ran forward frantically.

The fish house wasn't the one the boys were in, but that didn't matter. The fish houses had been arranged on the ice in rows. All he would have to do was to go along the row until he came to the one with the light.

The snow slackened slightly, and Danny saw the faint white glimmer of light a short distance ahead.

Praise God! The boys were in the next fish house!

Summoning new strength, Danny dashed forward until the depth of the snow once more robbed him of strength. He floundered forward and stumbled weakly against the door.

Inside, Jim Morgan sat bolt upright. "What was that?" he cried.

"Just the wind," Tom answered. His own despair had crept into his voice.

"No, it wasn't the wind. It was something else." Jim got to his feet and started for the door.

The rattling noise came again.

"There is something out there!" Jim leaped forward and jerked the door open. "Danny!"

The youthful pilot staggered into the little shack and for a moment rocked back and forth uncertainly.

"Danny!" Boyd Patterson and Tom Channing sprang to his side. "Danny! Are you alright?"

They guided him over to a bed near the stove and he sank weakly onto it.

"Are you alright?" Joe Cook repeated.

"I–I think so."

"Boy!" Matt exclaimed; relief evident in his face. "I didn't think you were *ever* going to come back."

Danny managed a weak little grin, although he was shaking violently. "For a couple of minutes or so – I was beginning – to wonder about that myself."

"We were afraid you'd fallen and gotten hurt," Boyd said.

"What happened?" Matt Dunlap wanted to know. "Were you lost or something?"

"How are we going to get out of here?" Joe Cook demanded.

"Lay off, will you?" Jim said. "Danny doesn't feel like talking right now. Give him something hot to drink, and something to eat, too!"

Danny leaned back and closed his eyes, breathing heavily.

Jim hovered over him uneasily.

"Do you feel alright, Danny?" he asked. "You didn't get hurt or anything, did you?"

The youthful pilot opened one eye, and then the other. "I'm all right," he managed.

"Come on, Boyd," Jim Morgan said, "and help me get Danny out of these heavy clothes."

"OK."

While the two of them got Danny's boots and heavy coat off and wrapped a couple of wool blankets around his shoulders, Tom Channing prepared a pot of tea for Danny, then built up the fire. He put another log in the airtight heater and opened the draft slightly.

Meanwhile Matt and Joe opened and heated a can of soup for Danny, and toasted a couple slices of bread over the fire for him.

It wasn't long before Danny had almost completely stopped shaking. He opened his eyes and sat up.

"Boy, we were scared when you didn't show up," Tom Channing said. "We didn't know whether you were all right or not."

"I'm OK now," he said. "At least I think I will be if I ever get warm again." He took a deep breath and with great effort expelled it. "I'd forgotten that a guy could get so cold. I was so cold I felt as though I couldn't stand it for another minute."

"Cold or not, you sure looked good when you came stumbling inside," Jim Morgan said, laughing his relief.

Nobody else said anything.

"Whoever it was who got the idea of putting that lantern out to help me locate you sure had a good idea," Danny said after a time. "I would have had plenty of trouble finding the right fish house if it hadn't been for that light."

Matt Dunlap glanced in Jim's direction. "I guess we have to give Jim credit for that. As soon as we realized there was a good chance you were lost, he said we had to get a fight outside so you could see it if you happened to get close by."

"I got that idea from Dad Orlis," Jim Morgan replied. "Remember how he used to pound that sort of thing into us, Danny?"

"He sure did."

They listened momentarily to the storm.

"Sounds as though it's getting worse," Boyd observed.

Danny Orlis nodded. "You guys wouldn't have been able to get all the way to Garrison in this storm. I'm glad you were wise enough not to start."

"It wasn't a matter of being wise," Jim said, laughing. "We got ourselves gloriously stuck. And while we were trying to get the car out of the snowdrift, the blizzard struck. We didn't have a chance of getting out of here."

"We thought you might've fallen and broken a leg, Danny," Joe Cook said, "but Jim wouldn't let us go out and try to find you. He made us stay in the fish house."

Danny smiled his approval. "All the time I was out in the storm I kept thinking about you guys, and wondering what you were trying to do about me. I was afraid that you'd realize I was lost and try to come out and find me."

"I could hardly stand to think of your being lost out in this storm while we sat here and didn't even make an effort to find you," Joe continued.

"If you'd tried to find me, the chances are we'd be in a worse mess right now. We might have had three or four lost on the ice instead of just one."

Joe Cook pulled his chair close to the stove and extended his hands to warm them. It was obvious that he had something on his mind, but it was some time before he spoke. Finally, he turned to Danny.

"What I want to know," he began, "is how are we going to get out of here, Danny? The storm seems to be getting worse all the time."

The youthful pilot smiled reassuringly.

"There's no sweat about that. We just sit it out until the blizzard's over."

"What then?"

"As soon as the weather calms down a little, the resort owner will send someone out to get us. That's part of his service."

Boyd Patterson's eyes widened, and he came over to stand before Danny.

"But how're they going to know that we're here?" he asked.

"That's one of the reasons they charge a dollar for each car that drives out on the ice and insist on registration. If a storm comes up or a fishing party doesn't come back when they're supposed to, someone can go out and find out what the trouble is.

"But we didn't register." The words were empty and hollow.

"You didn't register?" Danny Orlis echoed.

"No, we figured that you had made all the arrangements for the fish house, so we didn't have to register."

A tense hush fell over the little group. For some time, no one spoke.

"Then nobody knows that we're out here," Danny said numbly. "Nobody at all!"

CHAPTER 8

"THE ICE IS BREAKING UP!"

Conversation in the fish house choked off suddenly. Silence closed over the little group, a silence broken only by the heavy breathing of the boys and the muffled whine of the storm outside. In the dazzling light of the gas lantern the boys stared from one to another, questioningly.

"If nobody knows that we're out here, no one will come out after us, will they?" Jim asked of no one in particular.

"That's about the size of it," Danny said. "At least they won't be out here as soon as they would be otherwise."

"That doesn't sound very good," Tom Channing put in.

Silence again.

Joe Cook cleared his throat as though to speak but paused and tightly shut his lips as though to lock in the words.

"Better close that draft," Danny said at last. "We're going to have to stretch out our firewood to make it last as long as possible."

Matt went over to the stove and did as Danny suggested. He turned at last to the youthful pilot and slowly voiced the question that stood, unspoken, on every tongue.

"What are we going to do now, Danny?"

Danny Orlis did not reply immediately.

"That's something we've got to think out," he said finally.

Joe's hands began to tremble perceptibly and sweat ringed his face. It was an effort for him to speak.

"We're not in any real danger out here this way, are we?" he asked. "There isn't anything special that could happen to us, is there, Danny?" His voice choked off.

For the space of a minute or two no one answered him. Then his gaze found Danny's and held it forcibly. "We aren't in any danger out here, are we?"

The youthful pilot hesitated.

"Are we?" Joe's voice rose. "Are we, Danny?"

When Danny answered, his voice was calm and even. "We could be. There's always danger in a storm like this."

Joe Cook started. Fear flamed high in his eyes. "And what do you mean by that?"

"I just want to acquaint you with the truth, Joe," Danny went on. "That's all. I don't think there's anything to make our stay out here especially dangerous, but it doesn't do any good to ignore the truth, either. We're out on the ice a long way from shore, and the storm isn't letting up. In fact, it sounds as though it's getting worse."

Joe swallowed hard and began to chew nervously on his lower lip.

"I wish we'd stayed at home," he managed. "That's what I wish."

"It isn't going to do any good to talk like that, Joe," Danny said sternly. "We're out here and that's that. We've got to start from here and make the best of things. You asked me if this could be dangerous. I said that it could. I didn't say that we're in any danger now, or that we're going to be. But we must face reality. There is a possibility that danger could develop."

Jim Morgan pulled in a deep breath and expelled it in a thin stream. "We don't know how long the storm's going to last, for one thing."

"And for another, no one knows where we are," Boyd Patterson put in. "So, we can't count on having anyone brave the storm and come out after us."

Joe Cook jumped to his feet.

"The rest of you guys can stay out here if you want to!" he cried almost hysterically. "But not me! I'm going to get out of here right now! I'm not going to wait here and–and hope we don't get into trouble!"

Danny went over to him and grasped him firmly by the arm.

"Now, wait a minute," he exclaimed. "I know just how you feel. I'm not very keen on staying out here myself and I don't imagine the other guys are, either. But the best way I know for us to get into big trouble is to leave this fish house and start for shore in this storm. Believe me, I know what it's like out there! It's way below zero and the wind is so strong it would drive the cold through any clothes we would put on. There's so much new snow, we'd have to plow through drifts waist deep. And if that isn't enough, we couldn't see more than a few feet ahead. No sir, we wouldn't last half a mile."

Panic flickered in the basketball player's eyes. "That may be true, but it's no worse than sitting here w-w-waiting for trouble."

"Get hold of yourself, Joe!" There was no sympathy in Danny Orlis' manner. "Nothing has happened to us yet, and if we keep our heads and act intelligently nothing is going to happen to us." He breathed deeply. "There's nothing else to do except to wait for daylight and hope the storm lets up a little by then."

The boy's lower lip quivered, and it was all he could do to speak.

"Daylight is hours away," he said. "There's no telling what can happen to us by then."

"Daylight is quite a time away. We should make the most of it. Let's have a little time of prayer before we turn in and get some sleep."

"Sleep?" Joe exclaimed, shifting nervously from one foot to the other. "Who feels like sleeping tonight?"

"We may not feel much like sleeping," Danny told him,

"but we've got to get some sleep, just the same. There's no knowing what we'll have to do tomorrow, but there's one thing for sure. We'll have to have all the strength we've got. So we'd better sleep as much as possible."

"I think I'm tired enough to go to sleep, anyway," Jim Morgan said. "I didn't realize it, though, until right now."

"I think I can sleep, too," Boyd Patterson said, reaching down and untying the knots in his boot laces.

Danny took his Bible from his duffel bag and handed it to Tom Channing, who was sitting the closest to the light.

"Why don't you read something for us before we have prayer?" the young pilot asked.

"Have you got anything special you want me to read?"

Danny Orlis pursed his lips. "How about Psalm 91?" he asked.

"That's the portion of Scripture my dad always reads when we have serious problems," Tom Channing said. "He said it was his favorite when he was flying in Korea." He opened the Bible and began to read. "'He who dwells in the shelter of the Most High will abide in the shadow of the Almighty…'" As he continued to read, some of the fear seemed to go out of Joe's face, and for a brief moment a smile flitted on his lips.

The guys sat there, listening more intently than they had ever listened to a Scripture reading before.

When Tom finally finished Danny got to his knees on the rough board floor. Jim, Boyd, and Tom did the same. Matt looked at Joe questioningly, then went on his knees. After a moment Joe knelt as well.

"Our Father and our God," Danny began, "how we thank You for watching over us and caring for us thus far. How we thank and praise You for helping me to get back here safely. Now we want to talk to You about the fix we're in. You know that we're way out here on the ice, snowed in, and without any chance of getting help because no one in Garrison even knows that we're out here. But You know we're here, Dear God, and we're putting our trust in You to guide and direct us, and to help us get back safely to shore…."

When Danny finished, Boyd prayed, then Tom, and then Jim Morgan. When Jim finished praying there was an awkward silence before the boys started getting to their feet. Matt Dunlap was the slowest. He got up after a time and sat in a chair, hesitantly running his hand across his forehead.

"I always thought a guy had to have a prayer written down so he could read it," he said curiously.

Danny glanced at the Christian boys who were with him and waited to see what they had to say.

"That isn't what the Bible tells us," Boyd Patterson said. "It tells us to 'be anxious for nothing, but in everything by prayer and supplication with thanksgiving let your requests be made known to God.' "

"What does that mean?" Matt persisted.

"It means that we're not supposed to worry about things. We're supposed to ask Him for what we need.

And that's just what we did tonight. We told him about the predicament we're in, asked Him to help us, and thanked Him for His promises to help us."

Matt Dunlap's forehead furrowed questioningly.

"But you didn't even sound as though you were praying," he went on. "You sounded to me as though you were just talking to God."

"That's what prayer is, Matt," Tom Channing put in. "God tells us in His Word that He wants us to come to Him in prayer and tell Him what we need. It's just talking to Him."

The other boy did not question Tom, but it was obvious that he was not entirely satisfied with the answer.

"The Bible says that where two or three are gathered together in His name, He will be with them," Jim said. "And in another place we're told: 'Ask, and it will be given to you; seek, and you will find; knock, and it will be opened to you.' All through the Bible there are promises that God will answer our prayers, and that He wants us to pray."

"And," Danny said, "praying is largely asking God to help us, and praising and thanking Him. It's really just talking to God, if we can say that reverently."

"And you really think it helps to pray?" Joe Cook asked.

"I know it does. I've had hundreds of prayers answered – big ones and little ones."

Doubt still stood in the Cook boy's eyes.

"We've prayed," he said, fear still straining his voice. "But God hasn't answered our prayers."

"He will." Danny Orlis spoke confidently. "That is one thing we can be sure of. The Bible says He will answer our prayers, and the Bible does not lie."

"Then you think that, just because we prayed, God is going to watch out for us and help us to get out of here safely?"

"If it's in God's will for us," Danny said, qualifying the statement.

"And what do you mean by that?" Joe continued. "Is God going to answer our prayers, or isn't He?" I don't see that His will has anything to do with it."

There was a short silence.

"Tell me, Joe," Danny said abruptly, "when you were little and you asked your parents for money to buy candy, did they answer you?"

"Why, sure."

"Every time?"

"Of course, they answered me every time I talked to them."

"Did they always give you the money you asked for?" Danny asked.

"No kid gets money for candy every time he asks for it," Joe said irritably. "But I don't see what that's got to do with it."

"Could you say that they didn't answer you just because they said no?"

"I–I guess not."

"It's the same way with God. Sometimes He says yes, and sometimes He says no, and there are other times when He says, 'Yes, but I want you to wait awhile.' It might be that He has something He wants to teach us. It might mean that He wants to use the waiting period to get something out of our lives that shouldn't be there, or to teach us to be patient. He might even have something He wants to teach us by saying no to our prayers."

Danny went over and put another length of wood in the heater before continuing.

"If you'll remember, when I prayed, I asked God to give us safety and so on, if it was in accord with His will for our lives. You see, He always answers according to His plan for our lives. He doesn't promise to make things easier for us."

Joe Cook's frown deepened. "I don't get it. I don't get it at all."

He took off his boots and set them carefully beside his sleeping bag. Danny waited for the space of a minute or two, waiting to see if Joe would pursue the subject further, but he did not.

"Of course," the young pilot said, "there is a prerequisite before God can answer prayer."

"And what's that?" By this time Joe had undressed and crawled into his sleeping bag.

"There is only one promise in the Bible that God makes to answer the prayer of an unbeliever. That is, 'God, be merciful to me, a sinner!' And when it gets right down to it, that's the most important prayer a guy can pray in his entire lifetime."

Joe raised on one elbow; his eyes boring into Danny's.

"The Bible tells us that we all are sinners," Danny continued, "and that God hates sin so much He cannot even look upon it. It tells us that the sinner is going to Hell unless he has confessed his sin and put his trust in the Lord Jesus Christ to redeem him. So, the most important prayer we can pray is that of forgiveness."

Joe Cook's face was ashen and his lips thin and blue. He cleared his throat as though to speak.

"Yes?" Danny asked encouragingly.

"Oh–oh, nothing." Joe lay back down and closed his eyes.

"Want me to turn out the light, Danny?" Tom asked, after a moment.

"I think so." Danny spoke with great reluctance. But it was no use waiting for a response from Joe. The frightened boy had closed the subject decisively.

Danny crawled into bed while the gas lantern grew dimmer and finally went out. For a long while he lay there, eyes closed, considering their situation. He had been ice fishing many times before. He had been stranded on the ice in storms of varying intensity, too, for that matter. It had never seemed to bother him a great deal on those other occasions. It was strange that he should be so apprehensive now.

Slowly he raised on one elbow and peered into the darkness. For one thing he wasn't alone this time, nor did he have anyone his own age. He had the responsibility of caring for the boys. To be sure, they were all in high school and were almost as big as he was. But they wouldn't be out on the ice if it hadn't been for him. And they were looking to him for guidance.

Keeping them calm was going to be the big problem if the storm was still raging when they got up in the morning. That, and getting them off the ice before they ran out of food or wood for the heater.

If only Boyd and Tom had checked in with the resort owner at Garrison as they were supposed to. But, again, that was his fault. He told them about it, but only casually. He should have gone into detail, explaining its importance.

If they would just go to sleep for a few hours, that would help some.

Deliberately Danny lay back and closed his eyes once more. He had to get some sleep himself. That was for sure. There was no knowing what they would be called upon to do, come daylight. His experience out on the ice earlier in the evening had drained his powerful body of strength, and he lay there, exhausted.

How long he lay there he did not know. Time seemed to blur, one hour into another. Now and then he drifted off to sleep, fitfully, only to awaken after a few minutes. Joe Cook wasn't the only one who was concerned about their being stranded on the ice. In spite of Danny's efforts to leave it with the Lord, worry continued to pry at the corners of his mind.

Whenever he awakened, which was often, he could hear the storm raging outside. An hour or so after he found his way back to the fish house, he had thought the wind wasn't blowing quite as hard as it had been, but he realized now that only his imagination had made it seem so. He could hear the dismal howling of the wind as it roared across the icy wastes. He could feel it as it buffeted the shack.

It was probably still snowing, but it wouldn't matter a great deal one way or another as far as visibility was concerned, or the drifting of the snow. Enough new snow had fallen for the wind to create a ground blizzard of staggering proportions. The drifts were already deep enough to be all but impassable.

He had to get the boys off the lake safely, and as soon as possible. But how? How?

Silently Danny Orlis began to pray for God's strength and wisdom in knowing what to do. He was still praying when he heard Jim Morgan roll over suddenly and sit up.

"Hey, Danny!" Jim cried. "Danny!"

The young pilot opened his eyes, straining into the darkness.

"Yes?"

"Is it wet over where you are?" Jim asked.

"Wet?" Danny echoed. "Why would it be wet?" "That's what I'd like to know."

"Is it wet over there?"

"It sure is. My bedroll's getting soaked."

Danny Orlis reached for the flashlight and switched it on. The water stood three inches deep in the opposite end of the fish house!

His entire being chilled.

There was only one explanation!

The ice around them was breaking up!

CHAPTER 9

INTO THE STORM AGAIN!

Back in Fairview, Kay Orlis sat in the living room with Linda Penner. Becky came in from the kitchen and plumped herself on the sofa.

"Oh, Kay!" she exclaimed, her eyes widening, "it's snowing something terrible outside."

"I know." Kay was trying hard to keep from thinking about the storm.

"Do you know you can't even see the streetlight?" Becky continued. "The snow's blowing so badly I could hardly see the light on the front porch when I turned it on.

Kay put her arm about Becky and smiled down at her. "I'm glad we're in where it's nice and warm, aren't you?"

"I sure wish Danny and Jim hadn't gone fishing. They're apt to be awful cold if they're outside in a blizzard like this."

"I'm sure they're not outside, Honey," Kay said comfortingly. "You see, Danny knows a lot about storms.

When it started to snow, he'd get Jim and the other boys inside. He wouldn't let them stay out in a blizzard."

Linda Penner's lips curled petulantly. "I'll bet Danny and Jim and the rest of the guys are wishing now that they'd stayed at home. Of all the stupid things anyone ever heard of doing, ice fishing is absolutely the worst. If they did get caught out in the storm it would be just what they deserve."

Kay acted as though she hadn't heard her.

Becky sat beside Kay, frowning pensively. "If Danny can't take care of Jim and the boys, Jesus can," she said, smiling suddenly.

"That's right." Kay squeezed her affectionately. "Jesus can take care of them. And we know that He will take care of them, don't we?"

"If we pray and ask Him to."

"I was just thinking that myself."

Kay Orlis slipped to her knees beside the sofa and Becky joined her, simply, trustingly.

Linda snapped her book shut and got to her feet.

"Well, pardon me!" she exclaimed, sarcasm tinging her voice. "If you're going to turn the living room into a prayer meeting, I'll leave."

"We'd like to have you join us," Kay told her.

"Thank you, no." She stomped into her bedroom and slammed the door.

Becky Penner prayed first, as though she were talking to a dear and trusted friend. She told Jesus about Danny and the boys going ice fishing and about the terrible storm that had hit. "…and Kay and I are so worried we just don't know what to do," she continued. "Linda's worried, too – I think only she wants to act like she doesn't care. We'd like to have You look after them, Dear Jesus. Please take care of them and help them to get back home safely…."

When she finished praying, Kay prayed.

Becky jumped to her feet again, her tiny face glowing.

"Now we don't have to worry anymore," she said in complete confidence. "Jesus is going to take care of them."

"That's right, my dear," Kay answered, "Jesus is going to take care of them."

She knew that was true. She kept reminding herself of it at various times during the evening. However, she could scarcely keep from being concerned. Danny was used to the north and its storms, that was true. And he knew how to take care of himself as well as anyone, but this storm had struck so suddenly and almost without warning. It was entirely possible that the storm had caught them out on the ice.

It would be foolish to call, she told herself, but at least if she did get Danny by phone, she would be able to rest easily that night, just knowing that they were all safe and well.

She got up resolutely and went into the other room to call Danny in privacy.

Kay pressed Danny's speed dial number and waited for his phone to ring. The call, however, could not be completed for some reason. Kay tried again with the same result.

Kay went to bed then and drifted off to sleep, but from time to time she awakened fitfully to lie there, staring up at the ceiling. Near morning her feeling of concern grew until she could stand it no longer. She got out of bed and knelt in the cold room to pray.

"Dear God," she began, "I don't know where Danny is, exactly, or what he and the boys are doing, but somehow, I've got the feeling that they are in great danger. Please, God, watch over and care for them…."

* * *

In the fish house on Lake Mille Lacs Danny Orlis stared at the water that was coming up in the far corner of the little building.

"Wh-what's happening, Danny?" Jim Morgan demanded, his voice breaking.

Tom Channing awakened and sat up.

"What's the matter, you guys?" he cried. "What's happening?"

"The fish house is sinking, that's what!"

"Jim!" Danny switched off the flashlight and turned toward the Morgan boy sternly. "That's enough of that kind of talk. If you aren't careful, you'll panic everybody, including yourself."

"You saw the water yourself, Danny! You know that's what's happening."

By this time everyone was awake.

"What's wrong?" Matt Dunlap wanted to know. He sat up slowly and nibbed the sleep from his eyes.

"Yes," Boyd put in, "what's going on that you're all awake in the middle of the night? Has it quit snowing or something?"

"There isn't anything to get alarmed about," Danny Orlis replied, taking great effort to control his voice so he would sound no more excited than if he had just caught a sizable fish. "There's a little water coming into the fish house, that's all."

"That's all!" Joe Cook cried in desperation. "Y-y-you mean the f-f-fish house is going to s-s-sink?"

"I don't mean anything of the kind." The young pilot was stern. "We'd better get up right away and get dressed. That's all."

He didn't have to urge the boys a second time. They were already out of their sleeping bags. Their teeth chattering, they pulled on their trousers and heavy boots.

Danny was the first to be dressed and, while he waited for the others, he sloshed through the rising water to the table where the gasoline lantern was sitting.

Joe Cook joined him, teeth chattering and voice glazed with fright.

"The ice is breaking up, isn't it, Danny?" he asked numbly. "That's why the water is coming up in here, isn't it? The fish house is going to sink and we're going to sink with it!"

Danny grasped him by the shoulder and squeezed savagely.

"Joe, you've got to get hold of yourself. You're not going to be any good to us or yourself if you keep that up. We don't know that the ice is breaking up. We don't know for sure what's happening. But I can tell you this much. We're not going to sink in this fish house."

"I thought you said that God answered prayer!" the boy said bitterly.

"He does."

"Look what's happened to us!"

"What has happened to us?" Danny asked crisply. "Nobody has been hurt, have they?" The young pilot struck a match and lit the gas lantern. For an instant or two it flickered weakly. "We'll talk about that when we get back to Garrison, Joe."

"If we get back," the boy muttered under his breath.

Danny opened the jet and brilliant white light flooded the little fish house garishly. In spite of himself, he gasped and his heart chilled as he stared at the stark scene before him.

The water was already six or eight inches deep along one side of the building, which was listing badly. At any minute the ice on which they were standing could break in two.

"Everybody ready?" he asked.

Matt Dunlap's voice cracked.

"I am."

Jim looked about and spoke up quickly.

"I think we all are."

The boys crowded around Danny Orlis, concern clouding their young faces. Matt was the spokesman for them all.

"Wh-what are we going to do?" he asked. "Where are we going to go?"

"We've got to get out of here just as quick as we can," Danny ordered, his voice reflecting more confidence than he felt. "We've got to make it to shore."

"In this storm?" Jim Morgan echoed.

"We can't wait for it to let up." Danny went over to his sleeping bag and jerked out the heavy blankets he had in there. "Has anybody got a knife? Start cutting these blankets into strips about three inches wide."

"What are we going to do with them?" Boyd Patterson asked. Although he questioned Danny, he already had his pocketknife out and was doing as the youthful pilot had directed.

"We're going to tie ourselves together the way mountain climbers do."

Joe Cook's eyes widened incredulously and Danny saw terror that bordered on hysteria gleaming there.

"What good will that do, Danny?" he asked tremulously. "It won't help us get back to shore."

The calmness in Danny's voice when he replied helped to quiet the nearly hysterical lad.

"Of course it will help us," he said. "It'll help us to stay together when we get out on the ice. And, if we can stay together, we'll get to shore without any trouble."

Tom Channing glanced in their direction.

"I've got enough blanket strips now, I think."

"We'd better get a move on," Jim Morgan said, his voice quavering. "The water's getting deeper in here all the time. We don't know how long this old fish house is going to stay afloat."

Danny glanced a warning at him. "We'd better quit talking, Jim, and get these blanket strips tied together so we can get out of here."

Five pairs of eager hands snatched up the strips of blanket and began to tie them together hurriedly.

"Check those knots," Danny cautioned. "We don't want one of them coming untied when we get out on the ice."

"You can say that again," Boyd Patterson retorted, laughing nervously.

"That should be long enough," the youthful missionary pilot said at last. "Now line up and we'll get ourselves tied together so we can get on our way."

Joe Cook's hands trembled so badly he had difficulty in tying the improvised blanket rope about his waist.

"I–I know that we can't stay here," he mumbled, "but I–I sure do hate to think about going out in that–that storm."

Matt Dunlap echoed his agreement. "You can say that again. Just listen to the way that wind's howling."

Danny Orlis was paying no attention to what the boys were saying. He had taken his compass from his tackle box and had laid it on the table beside the lantern.

Boyd Patterson took half a step toward the door.

"Come on, guys," he said. "Let's get a move on. We haven't got all day."

But Danny wasn't ready to leave. "Just a minute. We've got to check our directions first, so we are sure we know which way to go."

"That's easy," Matt put in. "All we've got to do is to head for Garrison."

"But which way is Garrison, silly?" Jim Morgan asked irritably. "That's what Danny means. It's still dark out there and probably still snowing and blowing plenty. It's not going to be too easy to find our way."

"That's right," Danny said. "This old lake is mighty big for us to be wandering around on it without knowing exactly where we are and where we're going."

He turned the compass until the needle pointed to the magnetic north, then backed off to allow for the variation locally.

"We came out here," he said, talking more to himself than to his companions, "due east from Garrison. That means that we'll have to head due west in order to get off the lake in the shortest possible time."

"We could follow the road plowed by the resort owner," Boyd Patterson suggested. "It runs as straight as can be from here to Garrison."

"That would be all right," the youthful pilot said, "if the wind and snow hadn't been blowing so hard. Unless I'm badly mistaken that road will be one big drift from here to shore. And the chances are it's snowed in so deep that we couldn't even find it."

Jim Morgan looked down at the water which by this time covered the entire floor of the fish house. Over in the far corner it was more than a foot deep. Even as he stared at it, it seemed that the fish house lurched dangerously and settled another inch or two.

"Danny, we've got to get out of here!" he cried. "It's getting worse every minute."

"Let's bow our heads for a word of prayer," Danny said. Briefly he led them in a prayer of thanksgiving and a petition for strength, guidance, and safety. When he finished, he picked up the gas lantern and opened the door. "OK, guys," he said, "let's go."

They moved numbly toward the door.

"Remember this!" Danny exclaimed. "Once we leave this fish house we're committed! We've got to keep moving! We can't stop for anything!"

They nodded their understanding.

"OK. Here goes!"

Danny Orlis opened the door and stepped out into the raging storm. The fury of it staggered him.

The wind screamed at the boys from out of the north, hurling snow at them like pellets from a shotgun. It picked up the old snow, mixed it with new, and swirled it about them until it cut off their vision and filled their lungs, choking their labored breathing. Briefly Danny paused, fighting an all but uncontrollable urge to turn back.

"We can't go all the way to Garrison in this!" someone shouted. "We'll get lost and freeze to death!"

CHAPTER 10

"JIM'S IN THE WATER!"

Danny Orlis did not stop. He had to go on, and on, and on! He had to keep the boys moving – had to get them off the ice as quickly as possible. He knew, all too well, what was taking place.

Somewhere out on the lake, in one direction or another, the ice had cracked, allowing the fish house to settle dangerously. Or maybe…. Fear clamped its fingers of steel about his throat. Maybe the ice had cracked all around them. One could never tell about ice. In any event, somewhere on the lake, a great, yawning lead would be waiting – a strip of dangerous frigid water hidden by the storm to trap the unwary.

If he took the boys the wrong way, or failed to watch, even for a moment, for signs of danger, they could all become victims of the big lake. And the responsibility was all his. That fact lay heavily upon his heart.

But that was all the more reason for decisive,

intelligent leadership – all the more reason why he had to keep them moving. He squinted into the storm, trying to make out the shape of the ice and snow ahead. He pushed forward doggedly, one step at a time.

The rope about his waist tightened and he reached back and jerked savagely on it, a reminder to the boys that they had to keep moving. Even as he did so he prayed inwardly, in silent desperation.

"Dear God, help me to lead the boys in the right way. And help us all to get safely ashore."

He led the boys a dozen yards or so north from the fish house and turned at a right angle to head for Garrison and the safety of the shore. New snow had been falling steadily since he had made it back to the fish house some hours before. He knew that almost immediately from the depth of the drifts that blocked their path. But the wind wasn't blowing quite so savagely. Or so it seemed. It still drove the snow into their faces and whirled great clouds of it about them so that it hindered their breathing and combined with the darkness to keep them from seeing more than a few feet ahead. But it seemed to lack the wild, unrestrained, driving force of a few hours before.

Danny kept moving forward, not allowing himself or the boys to stop for rest. He floundered through the drifts and scrambled over the rough ice that had been swept bare by the wind. The boys behind him kept pace. The rope seldom grew taut between them.

Every now and then Danny stopped, got his

compass from his pocket, and checked their direction. It was too cold, and the going was too difficult to take a single step out of the way if they could avoid it. On these occasions the boys turned and hunched their backs to the wind.

"All right!" Danny Orlis would shout as cheerily as possible. "Let's go!'

After what seemed like an hour or so, but was probably only a matter of minutes, a dark barrier blocked their way. Danny stopped abruptly and his companions came up about him.

"Danny!" Boyd Patterson shouted above the roar of the storm, "What's the matter?" There was fear in his voice. "What's the trouble?"

There before them stretched a long ridge of jagged ice that had been thrown up in a line like a picket fence to bar their way. In the darkness they could just make it out.

"What're we going to do?" Boyd asked, once more raising his voice. "Are we going to try to go around?"

Danny glanced in one direction and then the other. Going around the ice barrier might be the wisest thing, but who could tell whether or not that was possible? The ice may have been thrown up that way for a hundred yards, two hundred yards, or several miles.

"Nope! We're going over the top!"

Before they could protest, he led them on, scrambling doggedly up the sharp ice cakes, over them, and into the drifts on the other side. He fell twice, cutting his hands and face. But he got to his feet and pushed on, more determined than ever to keep going.

Cautiously he shoved through the deep snow, eyes searching for the telltale ribbon of black that would reveal open water. In spite of the danger, Danny increased the pace as much as he dared. There was danger in not seeing a lead and stumbling into open water between two ledges of ice. There was even greater danger in remaining on the ice and risking the storm and sub-zero temperatures.

It was during severe windstorms that the ice buckled and broke up, that leads opened to trap the unwary. It was during storms when the wind was raging that most of the winter lake tragedies were set up. Danny was aware of all this, even as he was aware of the fact that this wind still gave no indication of slackening.

He began to pray inwardly once more.

As he battled forward, the boys in a line behind him, time seemed to stand still. The wind seared his lungs and set them aflame. The cold drove to the very joints and marrow of his bones. His feet were frozen stumps that had long since lost their feeling. The piercing cold had numbed his arms until they seemed queerly detached from his body. He had the strange sensation that it didn't matter what happened to his arms, that they didn't quite belong to him. A great, throbbing ache enveloped him.

Danny continued to slog through the snow. He had long since ceased to think. He was a machine, pushing forward step by step by step as though he was being driven.

Now and then one of the boys in his charge stumbled and fell. When that happened shortly after they had left the fish house, the unfortunate individual scrambled quickly to his feet, as though ashamed of his own clumsiness. As the minutes dragged by, however, saving face no longer seemed to matter. The boys still got to their feet again and pushed forward, but each movement was agonizingly slow and painful. Even the simple matter of getting on their feet again after they had fallen became a project. They were tired. Desperately tired.

After a few minutes Joe Cook stumbled and fell, jerking so hard on the rope he almost jerked Danny Orlis from his feet. For the space of a minute, he lay there, sprawled on the snow.

"Joe!" Danny cried, "are you alright?"

The boy groaned.

"Are you hurt, Joe?" he demanded.

Joe groaned again and turned wearily on his side. "I–I'm all right, Danny," he half whispered, "but I just can't make it! I can't go on!"

"Yes, you can!" Danny's voice was stern and decisive. "You can, because you've got to!"

Joe started to get up, but stopped and sank back to the ice.

"I just can't go on!"

Roughly, Danny grabbed him by the shoulder, and jerked him to his feet.

"We've had enough of that sort of talk from you! Let's stop this whining and get on our way. You can't quit now!"

Joe smarted under Danny's rough treatment but did as he was told.

"All right, guys!" Danny shouted above the roar of the wind. "On the double!"

Danny started off at a brisk pace, but after a hundred yards or so he slowed the pace briefly. He couldn't drive them quite so hard. There had to be haste, that was sure, but the boys were pushing dangerously close to the point of total exhaustion. He couldn't keep on driving them that way, or they would soon reach the place where they had expended all their strength and wouldn't be able to keep slugging forward. He had to let them rest.

Danny kept them moving at a slow, measured gait. They had to have a certain amount of rest. But only for a moment. Only until the burning ache started to go out of their lungs. Only until the strength began to come back into their tired bodies. There would be time for rest later when they were all safely off the big lake and in a house or cabin somewhere on shore. There would be time for them to stretch out later and sleep the pain away – when there was no danger from the elements. Now they had to keep moving forward without regard for the burning in their lungs or the throbbing in their legs and feet.

And it was Danny's responsibility to see that they did keep going. It was his job to see that they didn't get to feeling sorry for themselves and quit. If that happened, they were done! Finished!

Danny Orlis once more quickened their cadence.

"A little faster, you guys!" he shouted above the roar of the storm. "What do you think you're doing out here, anyway?"

He heard one or two grumbling under their breath.

That was good, he told himself. *Let them get mad at me. It'll keep them from thinking about themselves and the mess we're in.*

The thick impenetrable dark of night began to fade slightly. The change wasn't much. Not enough to be measured by the unpracticed eye, but to one like Danny, who had been born and raised in the wilds, it was unmistakable. His smile came back fleetingly, and the chill in his heart began to thaw a little. Their plight wouldn't seem quite so formidable in the daylight.

With the gray of dawn, the storm seemed to lose some of its fury. It wasn't snowing so hard and the force of the wind began to slack off. It came in gusts of varying intensity now, and when it lulled briefly Danny could see a short distance ahead.

His heart leaped with excitement during one such lull. Along the rim of the western horizon he could make out a faint, shadowy line. It was so dim – so indistinct – that he couldn't quite be sure of it. But it was there. He saw it again in a moment.

Trees! There were no islands in the north end of

Lake Mille Lacs. The sight of trees meant that they were not too far from shore.

Thank God! Thank God!

"Look, guys!" he shouted encouragingly over his shoulder.

"At what?" someone behind him called out.

"At the shoreline!"

There was a gasp and an answering cry of jubilation.

"Another twenty minutes and we've got it made!" Danny exclaimed.

The sight of land changed everything. It became a stimulant to their aching bodies, a goad to drive them on. They moved even faster than they had when Danny was crowding them. The rope behind him grew slack as the boys plunged through the drifted snow with renewed vigor.

The youthful pilot's heart sang. They were going to make it. They were–.

Danny Orlis stopped suddenly. His breath choked off. His very being froze. Once they had sighted land, it had seemed to him as though they were already safe. But no! At his very feet a crack in the ice revealed a narrow black stretch of water. The lead was narrow – only a scant foot wide – but it stretched in either direction as far as he could see.

He tried to speak, but there were no words. The boys came up beside him anxiously.

"What's the trouble, Danny?" Tom Channing began. "What's–" His voice choked off.

Matt Dunlap gasped. "Now we are in for it!" He licked his lips uneasily.

Even as they stood there, immobile, staring at the lead, it widened perceptibly.

"Wh-wh-what are we going to do now, Danny?" Matt demanded.

"We're going to get across before it gets any wider." Danny spoke calmly, despite the wild racing of his heart.

"We'll never make it," Joe said, his voice trembling "We–we'll never make it."

"We sure won't if we don't get going!"

A prayer welled silently in Danny's heart. *O God! Keep the ice from crumbling under our weight. And– and help us all to get safely across.*

Danny Orlis took a deep breath. "All set?" he called out. The boys nodded numbly. Their faces were ashen and the smiles that had lighted their eyes only moments before were gone.

Danny had thought of having the boys go first. He was the leader. He should be the last to reach safety. But doing that would mean that they would have to waste important time they did not have in order to untie themselves.

"I'll go first!" he shouted. "As soon as I get across, the rest of you follow, one at a time!"

Danny had Tom stand as close to the lead as he dared in order to give slack in the blanket rope, then he jumped. Although only a few tense seconds had passed since they first spied the open water, the lead had grown to a band two feet wide. Danny jumped it easily.

"Okay, Tom!"

Tom Channing crossed safely. Joe Cook was next. Then Matt Dunlap and Boyd Patterson. Only Jim Morgan was left.

By this time, the lead had widened considerably.

"Hurry up, Jim!" Danny yelled above the roar of the wind.

The younger boy looked down at the widening stretch of black water and hesitated.

"Come on!" Danny ordered. "That lead's getting wider all the time!"

The instant Danny Orlis yelled, Jim Morgan summoned all his strength and leaped.

Had the ice held, he would have made it. He landed with both feet on the edge of the ice shelf on the other side. But his weight and the force of his jump were too much for it. A small chunk crumbled beneath his feet.

"Help!" he shouted. "Help!"

And Jim Morgan slipped into the icy lake!

CHAPTER 11

MATT AND JOE'S DECISION

Jim Morgan struggled frantically in the icy water. "Help!" he cried out, terror cracking his young voice. "Help! Help!" With that his head disappeared momentarily beneath the surface. When he came up, his flailing arms hooked over the edge of the ice, where he clung in desperation.

For a brief, agonizing instant Danny Orlis and the boys stared in agony at him. Time was no more.

Boyd Patterson was the first to move.

"Take it easy, Jim!" he exclaimed, stepping forward with determination. "We'll get you out of there!"

"Don't come any closer!" Jim Morgan screamed in warning. "The ice is cracking. If you aren't careful, you'll all be in here!"

Quickly Danny took charge of the situation. His decisiveness belied his indecision of an instant before.

"Jim's right, guys!" he ordered. "Stay back and tighten on that rope!"

"Wh-wh-what're you g-going to do?" the boy in the icy water chattered.

"We're going to get you out of there. That's what we're going to do."

Obediently the boys moved back from the lead until the improvised blanket rope that bound them together was drawn tight.

"Now, pull!" Danny said crisply.

The boys dug in and pulled with all their strength. As they did so, Jim reached up on the ice with his arms as far as he could and tried to lift his weight.

"Pull! Pull!" Danny exclaimed.

Slowly Jim Morgan's slight body began to move out of the water. The ice cracked and popped ominously, but it held as the boys pulled him to safety.

Joe Cook gasped, "He's out! He's out!"

The guys slacked off, but Danny shouted an order to them.

"Keep going!" His voice was harsh and authoritative. "Keep going!"

Not until they had dragged him twenty feet or so onto solid ice did Danny allow them to stop. Then they came back and crowded around Jim excitedly. Matt Dunlap bent over him.

"Are you all right, Jim?" the other boy asked, his voice breaking.

"I–I'm c-c-c-cold," Jim managed between chattering teeth. "I–I'm awful cold."

Danny knelt beside him quickly.

"Are you OK?" he asked.

Jim managed a sick little grin. "I–I think so," he answered, "b-b-but I d-d-don't think I'll know for sure until we get someplace wh-wh-where my teeth stop ch-ch-chattering."

"We'll have you ashore in just a few minutes," Danny said. He peeled off his parka and threw it around the boy's violently shaking shoulders. "Here, put this on."

Jim shook his head in protest.

"I won't do it, Danny," he said firmly. "I'm not going to take your coat."

"I don't have time to argue with you. Do as I say!"

"But I–I can't do it, Danny," Jim continued. "It's j-just as bad for you to be cold as it is f-for me. I'll be all right as soon as I get in where it's w-warm."

Danny Orlis did not reply. Instead, he pulled the parka around Jim's thin shoulders and zipped it shut.

"You'd better save your strength, Jim," he said. "You're going to need it. We've still got a long way to go."

"B-b-but…"

Danny Orlis did not let Jim finish what he was saying. He helped him to his feet and started forward once more.

"All right, guys!" he sang out. "Let's get going! We've got to get Jim in where it's warm and do it pronto! There's no time to waste!"

He set the pace faster than he had before; as fast as he thought the boys could take and still keep moving. But they realized the urgency of the situation even as he did, and they moved fast enough to keep the blanket rope slack between them.

Now that Danny was without a coat, the sub-zero wind was brutal! Jim wasn't the only one who needed shelter. He had to get ashore and get in where it was warm himself.

The trees on shore were in sight almost constantly now and he could make out the form of a car on the highway. To the left he was able to distinguish the dim outline of the filling station on the edge of Garrison.

"Look over there!" he shouted triumphantly. "There's Garrison! We've got it made!"

A shout went up and the boys broke into a run. Danny's blood coursed excitedly through his veins, and, for the moment, he forgot how cold he was.

They were safe! Thank God, they were safe!

Someone in the filling station must have seen them about the same time. Two or three men came running out to meet them.

One of them dashed back for his car when he saw that Jim had fallen into the water, and another peeled off his own coat and had Danny put it on. Shortly after the half-frozen little group reached the road, the car came roaring up to get them and take them to the filling station and motel.

* * *

Some two hours later Danny and the boys sat around the stove in the office of the motel with the motel owner and several men and women from Garrison.

"Do you feel all right, Jim?" Danny Orlis asked anxiously.

The boy nodded.

"Since I got into some warm clothes, I feel all right. I didn't think I was ever going to get warm again." He shivered at the thought.

"Me too," Danny added.

"What I can't figure out," one of the men said, "is why the resort owner who rented you the fish house didn't come after you. That's part of the service in that dollar you pay for driving out on the ice. They're supposed to go out after you if the weather gets bad and you don't come in at the time you're supposed to."

"It wasn't his fault," Danny Orlis explained. "There was a little mix-up on our part. He didn't even know that we were out there."

Danny explained how it had happened that they hadn't stopped to report to the resort owner before going out to the fish house.

"I thought it was something we should look into if one of the resorts had left you out there knowingly."

There was a short silence. Then Danny turned to one of the men who lived in Garrison.

"I'm afraid we still have something of a problem,"

109

he said. "Boyd's car and the plane I flew over from Fairview are still out there. How are we going to get them off the ice?"

The stranger smiled.

"Now, don't you worry about that. Just as soon as the storm eases off a bit we'll go out and get them both for you."

"Thanks a lot," Danny said.

The wife of the motel owner insisted on fixing dinner and supper for them. The boys all slept awhile that afternoon and gathered in one of the motel units after the evening meal. But they were strangely subdued and quiet. All the roistering laughter and bantering were gone, and so was the horseplay. They sat around, talking in low tones. It was almost time for them to go to bed when Danny Orlis took the Bible from the dresser and held it in his hand.

"I don't know whether you guys have done any thinking about it or not," he began, his own manner serious, "but we certainly have a lot to be thankful for today."

Tom Channing nodded emphatically. "You can say that again. You can sure say that again! I wouldn't have given much for our chances out on that ice this morning."

Jim Morgan broke in quickly. "Especially me!" he exclaimed. "If it hadn't been for the Lord and His watching over me, I–I could have–I could have drowned when I fell in that icy water."

Danny Orlis' eyes narrowed as he looked from one to the other.

"That's right, Jim," he said, repeating it for emphasis. "That's exactly right. You could have drowned. But if you had, it wouldn't have been the terrible tragedy that it could have been if it had been someone else."

Matt Dunlap started. His eyes flamed accusingly.

"Now, what do you mean by that?" he demanded. "Isn't Jim as important as any of the rest of us?"

"Of course, he is," Danny replied. "If I am going to be completely honest, I suppose I would have to say that he means more to me, personally, than the rest of you boys. He's lived with us for so long, he's like a son to me."

"Then what did you mean by that bit about it not being so bad if Jim had died out there?" Matt went on, still bristling.

"Simply this. If someone who didn't know Christ as his personal Redeemer had fallen in the lake and had drowned, he would have been lost forever."

"I can't buy that," Matt broke in, his youthful voice harsh.

"I don't like to have to 'buy' it, either, but there's no choice for us. The Bible says, 'He who believes in the Son has eternal life; but he who does not obey the Son will not see life, but the wrath of God abides on him.' There's no way we can get away from that."

Joe Cook got to his feet uneasily. "You don't mean that God would send a guy to–to Hell, do you, Danny?" he demanded incredulously.

"No," the young missionary said, "God would not send a guy to Hell."

"I didn't think so."

"The Bible tells us that He is not willing that any should perish. But that doesn't change the fact that the person who has not met His conditions for eternal life will be lost. The Bible also tells us, 'For the wages of sin is death, but the free gift of God is eternal life in Christ Jesus our Lord.' In another place it says that we all have sinned and come short of the glory of God. So, you see, we all are sinners and have all earned the death we get."

Danny paused momentarily, to allow the full weight of the Scriptures to rest upon them.

"If a guy goes to Hell," he continued at last, "God doesn't send him, he sends himself. He goes to Hell because he loves his sinful life and wants to live that way. It's as simple as that."

Matt Dunlap looked at Joe and swallowed hard.

"I certainly had never thought of God as being so vengeful and–and harsh." His voice took on an edge. "I still think He loves us far too much to let us go to Hell."

Danny's gaze met his evenly.

"You know something, Matt. It doesn't matter much what you think, or what I think. The only thing that really counts is what the Bible says. The Bible tells us that God loved us so much He sent His Son to the cross to die for us. But it also tells us that He is a holy, just God and cannot tolerate sin. Since we are all sinners, the only way we can be with God is by getting rid of our sin. And the only way we can do that is by confessing that we are sinners and accepting Christ as our Savior."

The color drained from Joe's ashen cheeks, and he could not meet Danny's gaze with his own. He acted as though he wanted to speak, but he could not. He ran his hand nervously over his face and shifted from one foot to the other. The youthful pilot eyed him momentarily, then looked from him to Matt and back to Joe again.

"Did it ever occur to you," he began, weighing his words carefully, "that God might have spared us all on this trip just so you guys would have one more opportunity to be saved?"

Joe Cook's lips quivered, but it was Matt Dunlap who spoke with sudden resolution.

"It's something to think about, I guess," he said.

"We really should do more than just to think about it," Danny countered. "You can think about it until the day you die, and it won't do you any good – unless you actually come through for God."

Matt swallowed hard. "I–I'm not ready right now." Danny's gaze held his steadily.

"You might not get another chance."

Fear stood full in Matt's eyes, but still he shook his head.

"Now now," he said. "Later, maybe."

"And how about you, Joe?" Danny Orlis asked, shifting his attention to the other boy.

"I–I guess I want to think about it, too."

Danny Orlis could not hide his disappointment.

"We'll be praying for you both," he said.

www.ingramcontent.com/pod-product-compliance
Lightning Source LLC
Chambersburg PA
CBHW060503300726
48975CB00008B/2629